Innocently Guilty

Ashling Bourke

Innocently Guilty

Published by The Conrad Press in the United Kingdom 2021

Tel: +44(0)1227 472 874
www.theconradpress.com
info@theconradpress.com

ISBN 978-1-913567-54-5

Copyright © Ashling Bourke, 2021

The moral right of Ashling Bourke to be identified as author of this work has been asserted in accordance with the Copyright, Designs and Patents Act 1988.

All rights reserved.

Typesetting and Cover Design by: Charlotte Mouncey, www.bookstyle.co.uk

The Conrad Press logo was designed by Maria Priestley.

Printed and bound in Great Britain by Clays Ltd, Elcograf S.p.A.

For Granny Kay, I miss you greatly.
For Mummi, you are an inspiration.
For Mum, I'd be lost without you.

Party invites

It was a Sunday night, and we had some major party planning to do for Nicole's Sweet Sixteenth which was less than two weeks away.

'How about a Black and White theme?' Nicole suggested.

'Ohhh that sounds classy,' I replied.

'Check out this template I found for the invitations, it'll look even better with the Black and White theme too!' Emily said excitedly.

Nicole and I gathered around her iMac to see Emily's template of a black rectangle which looked like white fairy dust falling towards the invitation details.

'Hhmm… It needs something more… Can I have the mouse for a second, Emily?' I asked.

'Sure, go ahead.'

I brought out the colour toolbox feature and played around until I found a golden bronze colour.

'What do you think?'

'That looks so cool, Lottie! Thank you, people will definitely want to come now!' Nicole squealed with excitement.

'Aw what are best friends for!'

I hugged her whilst Emily pressed command s to save the file.

'Nicole, did you talk to your parents?' I asked.

'Yeah, it took some convincing, but they said they trust me. So, they've rented a cottage for the weekend and they'll take my little brother with them too. So, no parents allowed,' Nicole explained.

'You're so lucky, Nicole! There's no way my parents would let me do that,' Emily sulked.

'Don't get me started! Mine would go and "boogie" on the dance-floor, no matter how many times I tell them no one calls it that anymore,' I replied in disgust.

'Well, this is our chance to prove them all wrong! I mean what *could* possibly go wrong?' Nicole asked.

'Nothing! Cause you have the two best friends that everyone needs during a party crisis. Isn't that right, Emily?' I asked.

'Definitely! Right, how many of these invitations should I print out then?'

'Hhmm let's say a hundred?' I suggested.

'What? I told my parents I would just invite our year group around!' Nicole sounded like she was going to panic.

'Oh c'mon, Nicole, everyone knows you should always invite triple in case others can't make it,' I reassured her.

'Ok, I just hope they don't steal or break anything.'

'Nah, they won't. We'll make sure of it.'

'Oh, I almost forgot! I got all three of us makeup and hair appointments at Glitter Chic's straight after school, just before the party starts,' Nicole said.

'Oh My Socks! It takes ages to secure an appointment there!'

'Well, it was my parents' birthday present for me and how could I possibly say no to that?' Nicole asked.

'There's no way you could,' Emily added with a smile.

She handed us each a pile of invitations to hand out at school the next day during our free period at 11:00. I was standing outside the school library, waiting for those who were willing to actually study, to hand them an invitation. Several groups of students strolled by until I locked eyes with the one, I was really waiting for... Robbie Wilson. He was in the year above and was so dreamy with his curly "I don't care" bushy chocolate brown hair and hazel brown eyes. He was super fit too as he was on the swim team. I quickly fixed my hair and struck a pose as I held the party invitations in my hand for them to grab. His friends walked past, most of them ignoring me until Robbie took the invitation out of my hand and said:

'Thanks.'

'You're welcome.'

My first words to Robbie. Once he was out of my sight, I immediately texted the girls.

Later that day at lunch, I filled the girls in on what had happened.

'...And those were my first words to him... Even the way he took the invitation from my hand was so perfect and his skin was so smooth...'

'Eeek! Can't believe you got to finally talk to your crush! What are you gonna do if he comes to my party next week?' Nicole asked.

'There's no way he would come! He's from the year above remember?'

'You never know, he might. He did take an invitation after

all,' Emily added.

'That's true, yeah.'

Perhaps Robbie would come to the party after all? I wondered. One could only hope.

2

'Leave it with me'

The girls and I were standing by the Science corridor waiting for our next classes which were biology and chemistry.

'I can't tell you both how excited I am for tonight! It's gonna be a night to remember,' Nicole said excitedly.

'I'm so happy for you, Nicole! I really hope it'll be the best birthday you've ever had,' I said.

'Of course, it will be when I've got you both by my side.'

'Shh... Robbie's heading this way... Let's talk about our homework...' Lottie interrupted.

'What?' Nicole and I both said simultaneously.

'Yeah, so I really struggled with question five. How did you guys feel about it?' Lottie asked.

Nicole and I exchanged blank, confused looks until Robbie interrupted us.

'Hey... um... Lottie, could I speak to you about something?'

'Hey Robbie, of course. Excuse me girls.'

She stepped aside and placed her hand on Robbie's arm as she asked:

'What would you like to ask me?'

He touched his hair momentarily and cleared his throat.

'I was wondering if you wanted to go to the party with me later?'

'Yes, that sounds good to me.'

She twirled her ponytail as he continued.

'Why don't we exchange numbers and I'll text you later on, yeah?'

She slipped her hand into his trouser pockets, pulled out his phone and handed it to him for his pin-code. He entered it and then she typed her number in.

'Shall we meet at four?' she asked.

Nicole and I looked at each other in horror. How could she forget our Glitter Chic's appointment of all things?

'Works for me. See ya later, yeah?' he responded.

'See ya.'

She then returned to us but watched Robbie walk to the end of the corridor before screaming with excitement.

'Oh My Socks! Robbie actually asked me out! And he knows my name! I must be Cinderella in disguise.'

I gave her a smile whereas Nicole was biting her tongue. She was about to explode.

'Aren't you happy for me, Nicole?'

'I am but…'

I quickly interrupted.

'Of course, we're happy for you! Now you better get yourself to biology and update us at the party, yeah?'

'Yeah, of course. Right, see you both later.'

'See ya.'

I waited till Lottie entered her class.

'I know what you're thinking.'

Nicole sighed.

'It took me ages to secure that appointment and once again, she's gone and ditched us. Unbelievable honestly!'

'I know, it's just not fair.'

'Not fair? It's absolutely out of order when it's your best friend's birthday!'

'She needs to learn the true meaning of friendship.'

'What do you mean?'

'Don't worry, leave it with me.'

The school bell rang which meant it was time for chemistry.

Once school had finished, I asked Nicole:

'Is it all right if I meet you at Glitter Chic's at four?'

'Um... yeah but why? Where are you off to?'

'I forgot my shoes for tonight so, just quickly dashing home to get them. Is that all right?'

'Yeah, all right, I'll see ya later then.'

'See ya.'

I walked a few blocks till I found the corner where Chip was having a fag whilst waiting for me. He was wearing a large grey hoodie with grey gym bottoms and trainers with holes in them.

'All right, babe. How was school?'

'Boring as usual.'

'Come here, I'll show you what you've been missing.'

I walked closer till he grabbed my hand and pulled me in for a big slobbery kiss. After a few minutes, I pulled away and asked:

'Fancy going to a party tonight?'

'Thought you didn't want your pals knowing about us?'

'Well, I need your help with something.'

'Oh yeah? What does that involve exactly?'

'I need you to make sure a scene is caused… One where the person would make a real twat of themselves… You in?'

'Ok, who am I targeting exactly?'

'Robbie Wilson. You know him?'

'Oh, I do… I have just the thing for him.'

'Good. Oh, and remember, if anyone asks, we don't know each other, yeah?'

He sighed.

'Anything for you, babe.'

I leaned in and gave him one more smooch before heading off to meet Nicole. I had the biggest grin on my face as I thought of the evening ahead.

3

First dates

I ran home as fast as I could as I only had about forty minutes until I was due to meet Robbie for our first date. Once I got home, I immediately rummaged through my entire wardrobe for something decent to wear. I ended up deciding on a bright red crop top, black leggings and a black denim jacket with red converse. I had remembered an article that said red was the colour of attraction which meant that Robbie would find me irresistible. I topped my foundation, drew a thin layer of black eyeliner on the top of my eyelids and a blob of lip gloss on my lips. The time was 15:45 which meant I needed to head out or I risked being late which wasn't an option.

Ten minutes later, I found Robbie waiting for me just outside of Cookie Crush. He was wearing black jeans and a white button up shirt with black Ray-Ban sunglasses.

'Hey, you're looking good tonight,' he said.

'Hey, why thank you. You're quite dressed up for an ice cream date?'

'Well, I thought we were going to Nicole's party after?'

'Of course, we are.'

'Well, I'm just surprised by what you're wearing then.'

'What do you mean? Do you not like it?'

'No, I think you look great, but the invitation said it's a Black and White theme?'

Shoot, I had completely forgotten about that.

'Yeah, well, the girls and I have to stand out given it's her birthday, so the theme doesn't apply to us.'

'Oh right, that's all right then... Shall we go in?'

'Of course.'

He gestured for me to enter first just like a gentleman would. The café had a massive transparent counter displayed with a wide variety of ice cream options. It made it difficult to choose.

'Which flavours do you like?' I asked.

'I'm a big fan of chocolate and quite like the fancy ones too. What about you?'

'Oh nice, cookie dough is my absolute favourite.'

'Oh yeah, that's a good choice. Well, have you decided or do you need more time?'

'No, I think I'm ready.'

The shopkeeper glanced every now and then till she caught Robbie's signal that we were ready to order.

'Hi there, what can I get you?'

'Can I have one scoop of cookie dough and one scoop of strawberry please?'

'Yes, of course. And for you, sir?'

'Can I have one scoop of chocolate and one scoop of cheese-cake please?'

'Yes, of course. That'll be five pounds in total, please?'

Robbie grabbed a five pound note out of his wallet and

handed it to her. He turned to me and said:

'Don't worry, it's on me.'

'Oh, thank you.'

We both sat down in a booth near the shop window and a minute or two later, the waitress came to deliver our ice creams to us. We each took a scoop before I broke the silence with:

'So, how did you know my name exactly? We've never talked before today.'

'Oh, my neighbour is in your year, Taylor Johnson, I asked him about you, and he told me your name. I hope that's ok?'

'Oh yeah, of course. I just wondered really.'

'So, tell me something no one knows about you, not even your best friends.'

'Haha... What kind of question is that?'

'Don't know but everyone has their secrets which hide their real identities, I think.'

'Ok... um... Let me think... My parents really want me to become a lawyer, but I actually secretly want to become a fashion designer, but they consider that "a waste of brain power." What about you?'

'Ok, firstly, you don't have to do what your parents tell you to do once you're eighteen years old so, don't let that stop you from chasing your dreams and as for my secret; I really love gaming.'

'Oh, what types of games do you play?'

'League of Legends mostly... I've actually got tickets to go watch the professionals play next month which I'm very excited for.'

'Oh, that sounds great! I don't know how that game works exactly.'

'Well, you start by selecting your champion to play and they all have different abilities and roles. For example, Support does…'

I sat there nodding my head and saying 'uh huh' a few times whilst he talked about his game, as I thought about the number of times I've seen him getting in and out of the school swimming pool and smoothing his hair out. Butterflies were bouncing in my stomach until Robbie interrupted my thoughts with:

'So, what do you think of the game?'

'It sounds great! You'll have to show me it sometime.'

'Great, I look forward to it.'

He pulled out his phone to check the time and said:

'Oh, we better get going as the party will be starting soon.'

We grabbed our belongings and headed out of the café. He took hold of my hand and intertwined his fingers with mine as we took the scenic route towards Nicole's house. My cheeks were glowing red and my hands were sweating slightly as I wondered what it would be like to have Robbie as my actual boyfriend.

4

Party prep

As Nicole and I walked out of Glitter Chic's, we started walking towards her house, I turned to her and said:

'Nicole, you look absolutely amazing! I love the curls they've added to your hair, it really suits you.'

'Aw thanks Emily! I really like the eye shadow they've put on you, you should wear it more often.'

'If only they allowed us to wear makeup at school.'

'I know right!'

Nicole was quieter than her usual self as she confided:

'It feels weird not having Lottie with us... She would have loved getting a makeover.'

'Well, she made her choice... I'm sure we'll still see her at the party though.'

'Yeah, I guess that's better than nothing at least.'

We had just arrived at Nicole's house to find her parents packing up their car for the weekend.

'Oh sweetheart, look how beautiful you are!'

Greta greeted her daughter with a warm hug.

'Thanks, Mum.'

'Hello Emily, did you girls enjoy the makeover?'

'Hi Greta, we had so much fun, thanks!'

'Glad to hear it, where's your other friend-Lottie?'

'She was feeling a bit ill, so, she's gonna try and make it later to the party,' Nicole explained.

'Oh, what a shame! Hope she will be able to make it though. Now, are you sure you girls can manage all the party preparations? All the food is ready and waiting for you in the fridge and remember your guests can go in the garden too...'

'Mum, we'll be fine. When are you off to the cottage?'

'Just as soon as your dad has packed up the car! Oh, I can't believe my baby girl is already sixteen years old... I still remember when...'

Nicole interrupted.

'Mum! No baby stories please, you're embarrassing me!'

'Oh, all right, sweetheart. Right, you girls be careful and don't do anything stupid at this party ok? Mrs Granger next door will keep an eye out while we're away.'

'Don't worry, Greta, all will be ok.'

'Thank you, Emily. Right, that's us ready to go now, one more hug for the road?'

'Ok.'

The two of them had one more mother-daughter hug. Then, Nicole and I went into the house and put our belongings into her room. She turned to Alexa and asked:

'Alexa, play some music from my favourites please.'

'Ok, playing some music from your favourites,' the robot responded.

'So, what should we begin with? Party decorations?' I asked.

'Oh yeah, that's a good idea!'

Within two hours, the house had completely transformed into a Black and White party explosion from birthday banners to cupcakes and more. Nicole was wearing her favourite white dress with a black scarf tied around her neck and black ballet pumps whilst I was wearing a black tank top with a black and white chequered skirt and black ballet pumps too.

'This all looks absolutely perfect! I'm super excited now!' Nicole burst with excitement.

'This theme was a great idea, Nicole!'

Within the next ten minutes, people started strolling in mostly from our school and then a bunch of rowdy boys I recognised as Chip and his gang walked in with a cardboard box each filled with alcoholic spirits.

'Er… What is this? We can't have alcohol, we're under eighteen and who are you anyway?' Nicole demanded to know.

I gave Chip a stern look.

'Oh, c'mon Nicole! Can't have a party without alcohol and besides, I'm offended you don't recognise me, I attend your school too, you know!'

'Oh, sorry I've just never noticed you at school before but since you're here, you might as well stay.'

'Cheers, lass.'

Chip and his friends then headed into the living room to set up the spirits in accessible places for others. Adam from our year announced:

'Aw no way! Someone's brought alcohol! This party rocks!'

A crowd of people lifted cups and cheered with him.

'I'm not so sure this is a good idea, Emily, what if Mrs Granger calls the police?'

'It's all right Nicole, there's not that much and there's plenty of water and soft drinks that people can use to dilute the spirits with.'

'Ok, I just don't want to get into trouble.'

'Why don't we go chat those boys up some more for a drink, yeah? It's time to enjoy the party, not stress.'

'Hhmm yeah ok, you're right.'

I was grateful to have a chance to speak to Chip and ensure the plan was still going ahead.

The party

Robbie and I arrived at Nicole's house but just before we entered, he said:

'Lottie, I'm having so much fun with you tonight, I find you incredible.'

'Oh, thanks Robbie, I'm having a lot of fun with you too.'

He leaned down towards me, took hold of my head in his gentle hands and pursed his lips onto mine where it felt all tingly and mushy. After a few minutes, he pulled away, pushed a few loose strands of my golden curly locks over my shoulder and then took hold of my hand again as we entered the house.

It was jam packed with loads of people, either dancing, chatting or drinking from red plastic cups.

'Fancy a drink?' Robbie asked.

'Sure, I'll have whatever you're having.'

'Cool, I'll be back in just a minute or two.'

'Perfect.'

Whilst he was getting the drinks, I searched the crowd until I spotted Nicole and Emily talking to two rough looking boys

I didn't recognise from school. They were both wearing white tracksuits and were hovering around the girls like they found prey to pounce on. Nicole fortunately spotted me and gestured Emily to come and greet me. At least it got them both away from those boys.

'Happy Birthday, Nicole! The party looks great and I love what you've done to your hair!'

'Thanks, Lottie! How was your date?'

'It's been really great thanks, Robbie is just getting us drinks.'

'Did you forget the theme, Lottie?' Emily asked.

'Yeah, kinda, sorry! I was just so anxious about the date that the party theme… kinda slipped my mind… But I promise I'll make it up to you.'

Before we could talk some more, Robbie appeared with the drinks.

'Vodka coke, ok?' He asked.

'Yeah, that's great thanks! Robbie, let me introduce you to…'

I turned towards the girls to find they had disappeared; must be greeting other guests.

'Oh, sorry about that. Maybe we'll bump into the girls later on.'

'Fancy a dance instead?'

'Sure.'

Robbie grabbed hold of my hand and took me towards the dance floor in the living room where we both started bobbing and swaying along to 'Don't stop the party' by DJ P. I had never drunk alcohol before, but I liked the drink Robbie had made me, there was more to him than I initially thought.

'What's the plan?'

I pulled Chip to one side and asked:
  'Right, so what's the plan?'
  He pulled out a small plastic bag with white powder in it from his pocket.
  'Either get him to take this, which is bound to make him do something stupid or get him insanely drunk cause people always do stupid stuff when they're drunk.'
  'Ok… But how are you going to ensure he does either of those things?'
  'Is there like a place we can have a more exclusive party?'
  'We could try the attic. There's sofas and a table up there that we could use?'
  'That should do the job. Let's take some alcohol with us, too.'
  'Yeah, all right, follow me.'
  We each grabbed a few bottles and headed towards the attic which was upstairs. Once there, I pulled down the door using a hook tool and assembled the stair railings.
  'I'll go up first and then you can hand me the drinks, yeah?'

'Yeah, all right.'

Once we both got up there with the drinks. Chip set up the white powder onto the coffee table with a few rolled-up pieces of paper whilst I set up the drinks station using the cardboard box, they came in.

'Ah, we forgot cups!'

'It's all right, we'll be bringing the party crew up anyway, so, we'll get some on the way,' Chip explained.

'Who are you inviting up here anyway?'

'Just folk and Robbie, obviously.'

'Lottie won't leave Robbie's sight though and she'll find it odd if no girls are up here, so, I'll get Nicole to come up?'

'All right, just can't have too many people up here, as there's bound to be a snitch lurking around to the police about the drugs I've brought here. So, got to get the right people, if you know what I mean?'

'Yeah, I get you. Thanks for doing this Chip.'

'You owe me one, babe.'

I started walking backwards down the stairs and called out:

'I'll get the cups, you get the people, yeah?'

'Cool.'

I couldn't wait to see Lottie's face when she realised how pathetic Robbie really was.

The attic

Robbie and I had just finished dancing to our tenth song, a little bit of sweat was dripping down our foreheads and we couldn't keep the smiles off our faces until I surrendered with:

'Fancy another drink?'

'Yes, please!'

'Come with me.'

We were just heading to the drinks station when one of the boys I recognised from Robbie's group of friends stopped us.

'Robbie! Where have you been man?'

Was I invisible? I asked myself.

'Sorry Lewis, I'm on a date tonight,' Robbie said.

'Oh right, ok.'

One of the strange looking boys that Emily and Nicole were talking to earlier approached us.

'You boys been to the real party yet?'

'What do you mean, dude?' Lewis asked.

'The attic. VIPs only. You interested?'

'Hell yeah. Robbie, you and your date coming or what?'

'Um...'

He looked at me and I nodded.

'Yeah, we'll come.'

We all headed upstairs. The boy who invited us pulled down a step ladder from the ceiling and began climbing up. We followed suit to find a few couches, a small coffee table with lines of white powder and rolled-up pieces of paper. There were more bottles of alcohol available. I was surprised to find Emily and Nicole there. Is this where they had disappeared to?

'Right, two rules up here,' the party leader announced.

'First, no mixers allowed. VIPs drink spirits only.'

'Sweet man.'

Lewis started getting high fives from everyone to celebrate the rule.

'Secondly, we're not here to chat, we're here to play... That's why you've all been invited up here. So, shall we begin?'

'What are we playing?' I asked.

'First game is called Never Have I Ever... You'll need your drinks sorted first!'

I decided to expand my repertoire of drinks and so, I poured rum into my red plastic cup whereas Robbie stuck to vodka.

As the games went on, I began to feel invincible, yet the world was spinning in circles at the same time, that I failed to notice Robbie was trembling and cradling his head as though he was about to throw up.

'Bobbie! Are... Are you all right?'

'Yeah, I'll be fine... I just need the bathroom... I'll be back in just a few minutes,' he said.

'Ok! Don't take too long though!'

I watched Robbie go down the stairs but then every now

and then, I checked my phone for the time which was 21:30…
21:37… 21:43. Robbie still hadn't returned so, I decided to go
check on him. As I got off the sofa, I started seeing everything
and everyone in double and I could hardly walk straight until
Emily offered:

'Do you want some help, Lottie?'

'I need to find… Bobbie.'

'Who?'

'Bobbie… My date!'

'Oh, you mean Robbie. Let's check downstairs.'

Emily went down the stairs first and then guided me as I
descended backwards down the stairs. Keeping me steady until
I reached the bottom.

'Wha… Where… Where is he?' I asked.

'Let's check the bathrooms.'

We walked straight ahead towards the closest bathroom. I
knocked on the door and shouted:

'Robbie! Are you in there?'

There was no response. So, I tried opening the door handle
but the door was locked.

'Wha… What do… What do we do?'

'Wait, I'll get Chip.'

'Chip? No Bobbie is stuck… I don't want to eat chips.'

'Look, here he is,' Emily said.

Chip, the party leader arrived.

'Oh, your name is Chip! What a weird name that is!'

'Lottie, do you want his help or not?'

'Yeah! Open the door!'

'All right, move out my way.'

Emily and I stepped aside as Chip ran towards the door

with a blurry object and the door opened. I ran inside to find Robbie cradled by the toilet basin with vomit coming out of his mouth. He remained motionless.

'Robbie!'

Then, everything suddenly turned dark as I collapsed to the floor.

8

Plan B

'Chip! What the hell did you do that for?' I screamed at him.

'Emily, he's dead,' he responded.

'What? What do you mean he's dead?'

'Well, look at him. He's unresponsive.'

'Well, why did you hit Lottie then?'

'Because she would scream in terror and that would cause a commotion which would attract others… We need a plan B.'

'Well, what do we do?'

'Let's leave them both in here whilst we get everyone else to leave. Then, we can sort this mess out,' Chip said.

'I got this.'

I ran downstairs to the kitchen trying not to shed a tear to avoid questions and asked:

'Alexa.'

The robot paused the music for a second.

'Tell everyone they must leave the party now!'

'Ok, I will tell everyone they must leave the party now.'

There were a lot of boos and 'this party sucks' comments but pretty much everyone except those in the attic were leaving the house. Once I was sure they had gone, I went back upstairs and very quietly, I closed the attic door so they couldn't leave.

'Hey! We're stuck up here!'

I recognised as Nicole's voice.

Then, I went to the bathroom where I last left Chip.

'Ok, everyone except the party up in the attic are gone,' I said.

'Well, what about the people in the attic then?'

'I closed the door on them, so they won't be able to come down without us opening the door for them first.'

'Damn, I like it when you get bad, babe.'

'Not now Chip! We need to sort out this mess.'

'Oh yeah, we need to get rid of the body somehow.'

'Wait what! Lottie too?'

'I mean I know she's your friend and all, but she'll just tell the police on us.'

'I know she's annoying and not always best friend material, but I can't kill her… There has to be another way.'

'Oh, I just thought of something! We can use this situation to our advantage.'

'How so?'

'Follow me, I'll show you the plan. For now, you take her legs, I'll take her arms.'

We carried Lottie down the staircase as delicately as possible and laid her down onto the soft carpet floors of the living room and then headed back upstairs to get Robbie's body. We laid the two bodies next to each other and then Chip said:

'There, now we just leave them and when Lottie wakes up, she'll think she killed him.'

'No, we need something more.'

'What do you suggest?'

I left the room and snuck into Nicole's Dad's office, checked his drawers and found the dagger he kept in there for their family camping trips. I crunched-up a piece of paper from his printer, picked up the dagger with it and then, I returned to the living room to show it to Chip.

'Woah! What are you doing with that?'

I knelt down beside Robbie's body and shoved the dagger into his chest. Some blood started oozing out and then I grabbed a red plastic cup and made it spill near where Lottie slept to remind her of being drunk and backed away from them.

'There, it gives her more to believe that she did it. Now, we better join the others in the attic before they get suspicious.'

Chip flicked the light switch, so the bodies were left in the darkness. Then, we headed back upstairs to the attic.

'What happened downstairs?' Nicole asked.

'I think Lottie and Robbie drank a little bit too much as they passed out in the living room,' I explained.

'Oh, are they ok?'

'Yeah, they'll be fine, but we asked everyone else to leave so they could sleep, and the main party is up here anyway, so they don't really need to be here.'

'Oh, yeah I guess that's true... Someone must have shut the attic door though as none of us could get out of here.'

'Perhaps someone was frustrated they had to leave?'

'Enough of this. It's killing the vibe up here... Everyone, top up your drinks for the next round of games,' Chip said.

So, we did.

9

Frozen

Rays of sunshine passed through the window which irritated my eyes. I slowly opened them to find a blurry red blob in the distance that after a few blinks appeared to be a spilled red plastic cup amongst this soft snowy white carpet I was lying on. I tried to lift myself up, but my head felt like a hammer aiming for the nail. I could taste vomit in my mouth. I wondered what the point of drinking alcohol was. I felt my right-hand grab hold of something which I used to lift myself upright; a sinking motion had occurred. I cradled my head in my hands to steady the dizziness. Then, I asked myself what my right-hand was holding?

As I looked over my right shoulder, there he was… lying on his back… with streams of red blood gushing out of his chest from the dagger I must have used to lift myself up. He looked pale as a ghost. Tears suddenly dripped from my eyes whilst I spoke with trembling lips.

'Robbie? Can you hear me?'

There was no response. I took hold of his lifeless hand. I

looked around and found various people passed out on couches with those red plastic cups still in their hands. Several bottles of vodka, rum and tequila were scattered about. There were snores and grunts from the bodies, so they were alive at least. I looked back at Robbie, touched his face and mourned as an eruption of pain burst into my chest as the boy, I spent the night laughing, talking and having the best first date I could ever have imagined with was... dead... right in front of my eyes.

How did this happen? I wondered.

The events of last night were blurry as the taste of vomit crept up my throat. I couldn't bring myself to do anything other than cry. However, my stomach had other ideas.

I got up to run towards the bathroom to find Emily, by the doorway of the living room, in her blue fluffy jammies, slippers and a robe holding a warm cup of tea.

'Morning, how'd you sleep?' she asked.

'Sorry Emily, I really need the bathroom.'

'Go ahead.'

She stepped aside to let me through.

I ran towards the bathroom, opened and locked the door in a matter of seconds and knelt down towards the toilet basin to let all the vomit out.

Once I cleaned myself up, I unlocked the door and returned to the living room. Those sleeping bodies on the couches were gathering their belongings and rushing out of the door. I wasn't sure why they were in such a hurry to leave. Then, I saw the policeman kneeling down beside Robbie; examining his body. There was another policeman talking to Emily and jotting down notes on a small notepad. Emily pointed towards me and the officer came towards me; probably to ask me questions.

Instead, they spun me around and placed handcuffs on my hands behind my back and said:

'Lottie Sheldon, you're under arrest as a suspect for the death of Robbie Wilson. You have the right to remain silent and anything you say right now can be used against you in court.'

I looked over the policeman's shoulder at Emily who mouthed the words, 'I'm sorry,' then turned to let the policeman take me to the station.

Once we were at the station, they took my fingerprints, asked me various questions about my personal details and then, they informed me that they would contact my parents before my interview. Thank goodness, Father is a lawyer.

My parents arrived within an hour and rushed towards me to put their arms around me and tried to ask me what happened as though I knew the answers.

Officer Rodgers came towards us and said it was time for my interview. Father asked if he could accompany me as my lawyer which they agreed was ok. We were taken to a small room with three white plain walls and one transparent one. There was a wooden table and chairs. We sat across officer Rodgers as he asked:

'So, how did you become friends with Robbie Wilson?'

'We weren't friends… we simply went to the same school together… then, one day he actually noticed me and asked me out on a date.'

'What did you do together on the date?'

'We got some ice cream together and then went to Nicole's birthday party.'

'What did you do at the party?'

'The usual… drank some alcohol, chatted, danced… even

kissed a few times.'

'We found Robbie Wilson dead this morning as you might recall. Do you know anything about what might have caused his death?'

The thought of Robbie lying as pale as a ghost on the floor entered my mind followed by tears and trembling lips again as I said:

'I... I don't know... I can't remember... I just found him dead when I woke up this morning, that was all.'

'Ok. That is all we have to ask. You are free to go.'

'Thank you.'

When we arrived back home, I ran straight to my room, dug my head into my pillow on my bed and shut myself out from the rest of the world. Mother knocked on my door and asked:

'Lottie, sweetheart. Do you want to talk about what happened today?'

I stayed silent until she eventually got the hint and left me alone.

I checked my phone for messages but there wasn't a single one, not even from Emily or Nicole. Where were my friends when I needed them?

Everyone knows

It was Monday morning and Mother dropped me off at school. I didn't have the energy to do my makeup that morning and simply tied my hair up into a ponytail. I walked towards the main entrance of the school in a clean white button polo shirt, a swaying black skirt with black tights and black ballet shoes. I stopped by the school fountain next to reception which was where Nicole, Emily and I always met in the mornings. They weren't there though which was odd. Five minutes later, they strolled in through the entrance with their elbows interlocked with one another... and walked past me as though I wasn't there. I dashed after them, calling out:

'Emily! Nicole! Wait up!'

They stopped and turned around to face me.

'Sorry Lottie, we can't be seen with you. It would damage our school reputation,' Emily said.

'What are you talking about?'

They didn't answer. They just turned and kept walking towards class.

Did I do something wrong?

I continued walking to classroom B65 which was our registration class and sat down in an empty seat, avoiding eye contact with my classmates. A scrunched-up piece of paper appeared on my desk. I picked it up and opened it to find the word '*murderer*' written on it. I didn't know who wrote it, but every classmate avoided my glances which was enough for me to know that they all knew about the Robbie incident. I grabbed my bag and dashed out of the classroom hearing roars of laughter behind me. A few teachers tried to ask me where I was going but I just kept running till I was outside the school entrance. I grabbed my phone and dialled Mother's number.

'Hi Mum. Can you please pick me up?'

She arrived half an hour later and I immediately opened the passenger door and got settled into the car. Then I started to cry. Mother pulled the handbrake to stop the car, took her seatbelt off and reached over to give me a hug.

'What happened, sweetheart?'

'I just want to go home.'

I spent the rest of the week lying in bed staring at the corner of my chest of drawers. Whenever my parents tried to ask me a question, I stayed silent. I did eat sometimes but usually didn't have much of an appetite for food. My head was spinning with questions instead of answers to the one question I dreaded; did I kill Robbie Wilson?

By the end of the week, Mother arranged for Susan to come in, her therapist friend. She sat in an armchair across my bed and introduced herself:

'Hello Lottie. I'm Susan and I'm here to talk to you about anything you'd like to talk about, and this conversation will remain confidential unless another person is at risk. Shall we begin?'

'Sure.'

'Ok. Whenever you're ready.'

Fifteen minutes went by and I still hadn't said a word. Susan exhaled a breath of frustration and calmly said:

'Why don't we start with how you're feeling today?'

'Robbie is dead, and I don't... I don't know why.'

'How does that make you feel?'

'Lost.'

She jotted down some notes.

'Would you like to tell me some more about Robbie? What was he like?'

'No. I can't.'

There was a knock at the door followed by Mother.

'Sorry to interrupt, I just wanted to check how it was going?'

'Would it be ok if I came back tomorrow? I think we could do with some more time.'

'Of course, anything to help my little girl.'

Susan did come back the next day and the day after that as well.

'Do you remember what you did at Nicole's party?'

'The usual stuff... drinking... dancing... kissed Robbie a few times.'

'Do you remember passing out in the living room?'

'No, I just woke up... he was there... just lying on his back bleeding... Next thing I knew, I got arrested.'

Once again, Mother checked up on us. Susan stepped outside of my room to talk to her.

'It's been brought to my attention that Lottie is unable to

remember most of that night.'

'What does that mean exactly?'

'It means the brain refuses to be reminded of the events that occurred which suggests something incredibly traumatic must have happened.'

'What do you propose we do?'

'She needs to be able to switch her mind off completely from that night... It often helps to go somewhere that doesn't trigger the traumatic event.'

'Well, I have been meaning to take Lottie to Malawi for several years now to show her where I grew up as a child... But she is listed as a suspect so, would she even be allowed to leave the country?'

'Oh, how wonderful that you grew up there! I'm sure she would love that, and it would be such a diverse experience that would take her mind off the situation. As for the police, leave it with me, I'll talk to them,' Susan promised.

'Oh, thank you so much, Susan!'

I grabbed my phone and searched up Malawi and found various articles on malaria, HIV, villages... Why on earth would Mother want me to see that?

Summer camp?

It was lunch time at school. Nicole and I were eating our sandwiches when our phones vibrated with a text... a text from Lottie. Nicole grabbed her phone and read it:

'*Hey, just wanted to let you know, I'm spending my summer in a summer camp in Africa! Could my life get any worse? L x*'

'I'm worried about her, Em... She hasn't come back to school... She needs us.'

'Nicole, she *killed* Robbie Wilson. The police will lock her up in jail before she goes to a summer camp.'

'Well, I'm gonna text her at least.'

She typed a message onto her phone and sent it before I could ask:

'What did you write?'

'*Hey Lottie, that sounds exciting! Where did this idea come from?*' N x'

Seconds later, her phone vibrated again with a response:

'*A therapist suggested it. L x*'

'She's having therapy! Em, she's really struggling... Shouldn't we at least hear what happened? Maybe it was an accident?'

'No. You can't trust murderers. Who knows, we might be next on her list.'

'It just doesn't make sense… She's been crushing on Robbie for months so, why kill him?'

'I just can't believe she gets sent to a summer camp after committing a murder, since when does that happen?'

'At least she can have one more summer of fun before she gets locked up behind bars for the rest of her life.'

This was so not part of the plan. I kept to myself.

The arrival

A couple of months later, we landed in Lilongwe. The cabin crew did their usual announcements, not that I was particularly paying attention until the seatbelt signs went off. Everyone was frantically gathering their belongings to leave the aircraft. The moment I stepped out of the plane, there was a blast of humidity in the air. My hair felt ever so greasy as I desperately needed a shower. Mother, on the other hand, looked like she was ready for the beach. She wore a bright blue bow floppy hat with her long wavy blonde hair cascading down like a waterfall and a bright blue maxi dress that touched her ankles with black sandals. I was wearing bright red skinny jeans with a black tank top and matching flip-flops and of course, my favourite Ray-Ban sunglasses.

There was a bus waiting for all of the passengers. I turned to Mother and she gave me a calm smile as we entered the bus. It was crammed with people of all colours, shapes and sizes. Some casual looking, others in business suits. The bus strolled away from the aircraft to the airport entrance. A few minutes later, we arrived at the Lilongwe International Airport terminal.

First thing was passport control where everyone immediately rushed to a queue except for Mother and I. We went off to the side to fill in our details on a small piece of card. I looked at Mother and asked her:

'What are you doing?'

'I'm filling in an entry card to explain the purpose of our visit here in Malawi.'

Once she finished filling in the entry cards, we joined the queue for passport control. I could see we only had the option of seeing the immigration officers, no machines to let us through like we did back in the UK.

Geez, this could take a while, I thought to myself.

Ten minutes later, the immigration officer looked at our passports and entry cards. He looked at me, smiled and said:

'Ah, my son William will be at Camp Kulingana as well. He absolutely loves that place.'

Mother smiled and replied:

'That's wonderful! Maybe my daughter, Lottie here, will have a chance to meet him.'

I rolled my eyes at Mother. I still couldn't believe she was sending me to a summer camp in Malawi because Susan had suggested it would help... Robbie was dead and everyone claimed I did it and instead of jail, I got sent to a summer camp, I wasn't sure which one was worse?

When we got our suitcases, I was expecting to go through the "nothing to declare" door but instead we had to queue for the officers to look through our bags. I wasn't sure what they were looking for exactly, but they gave us the all clear. Then, we finally went through the exit door and it felt like being swarmed by paparazzi as there were Malawians everywhere. Some holding up names of the people they were collecting, others offering to help with our bags until we spotted a tall, hairy man holding a sign that said: "Camp Kulingana," on it. He was wearing a white polo t-shirt that had a small logo on his right of a baobab tree with Camp Kulingana written in red bold letters just above it in an arc shape. He also had knee length beige hiking shorts and curly brown hair.

He smiled and warmly introduced himself as Kyle and asked for my name and age. Mother said:

'Hi, I'm Leslie Sheldon. This is my sixteen-year-old daughter, Lottie Sheldon, who should be on the list for the camp.'

Kyle looked at his clipboard until he found my name and ticked it off the list.

'It's a pleasure to meet you both. I'm one of the instructors at Camp Kulingana. I'll let you two say goodbye before I take you over to the bus and then we'll get headed to the camp.'

He briefly turned away but then said:

'Oh, and don't worry ma'am, she's in safe hands with us.'

Mother replied with the biggest smile on her face.

'Zikomo.'

Kyle looked surprised and said:

'Ah, you know some Chichewa?'

Mother looked proud to be recognised as a local.

'Yes, I actually grew up here as a child and picked up some words here and there.'

I suddenly realised something, feeling a bit alarmed.

'How will I be able to contact you?'

'I've provided all the contact details the camp needs as I've been told phones are only allowed at specific times throughout the camp.'

'What? You're joking right?'

'I think it would be good for you to spend less time on your phone actually.'

I wanted to cry. How could my mother abandon me like this? She pulled me into a hug and very calmly said:

'You're going to have a great time sweetheart, make some friends, learn new things and more importantly see a different type of life than most of your friends back in England will experience this summer. I know it's a bit scary, but I wouldn't have sent you to this camp if I didn't think it would do you some good, ok?'

'Okay.'

Then, she looked into my eyes and said:

'Lottie, remember, there's no one here who knows what happened that night, so don't think about it too much and just have some fun.'

She pulled me into one last hug and handed me over to Kyle.

'Come on Lottie. It's time for you to go and start an adventure.'

Kyle took my suitcase as I waved to Mother one last time before we got to the bus. Kyle loaded my suitcase into the trunk of the bus and said I could go and get a seat. I looked over at him and asked:

'Um… Kyle, is there Wi-Fi on the bus?'

Kyle chuckled and said:

'No, sorry. I hope you've brought something to entertain yourself as it's going to be a pretty long journey if boredom hits.'

I sighed and sarcastically said:

'Great, thanks.'

I boarded the bus and suddenly several pairs of eyes were staring at me, some whispering as I headed to the back of the bus and sat down by a window seat all by myself. A few minutes later, Kyle got onto the bus and said:

'Ok everybody, I'm going to do a final headcount and then we'll be off. It's about a three-hour drive to Mangochi where the camp is so, make sure you put on your seat belts!'

I plugged my headphones into my iPhone and started listening to Ellie Nickel songs hoping the battery would last the journey.

As we drove along, I started to notice how there were no pavements for pedestrians next to the roads; it was all dirt and dried-up grass.

That's a bit unusual, I thought to myself.

Then, we stopped at a traffic light and I saw a small young Malawian boy in dirty ragged clothes holding up what looked like a stick with dead rats on it.

Eww, that's gross.

Not long after, I saw some Malawian ladies wearing some kind of patterned cloth around their waists and carrying a bucket of water on top of their heads.

How is that possible and why would they do that when they could just get bottled water from the supermarkets? I thought.

It was funny to see some chickens cross the road repeatedly as I couldn't stop thinking about the classic joke, "Why did the chicken cross the road? To get to the other side." I also saw a young boy with an older man guiding a herd of cattle with some sort of whip, just through the roads and edges like it was a perfectly normal way of getting them to their final destination.

But then, something really caught my eye: there were several little huts gathered in an area a bit like a neighbourhood which I assumed was a village. There were ladies cooking food with a small fire. Small young boys kicking about a ball of plastic bags wrapped together like a football. There were very skinny dogs hovering about. There were Malawian women of different ages pounding the ground with a tool that looked a bit like a hammer in some fields nearby. I knew people lived in villages, but this was not what I had imagined it would be like. A group of young Malawians looked up at the bus and started waving frantically and smiling. How could they be happy with a life like that?

I must have fallen asleep as I woke up to Kyle's voice declaring that we've arrived at the camp. The other campers rushed off the bus filled with excitement whereas I was hoping it had just been a bad dream I had. Kyle did another headcount and told us to follow him. I stopped and said:

'Wait, what about our suitcases?'

Kyle replied:

'Don't worry, they'll be taken to your bunks. Now, we're heading to the outdoor stage area where the directors of the camp will welcome you all so, you can settle in quickly.'

We all followed Kyle to this large field of trimmed grass where loads of campers were sitting facing a huge stage with the camp logo above just like the one on Kyle's t-shirt. I sat down where there was a space available along with the other campers that were on the same bus as me.

Suddenly, everyone grew silent as a tall bald white man appeared on the stage holding a microphone.

'Hello everyone and welcome to Camp Kulingana!'

Everyone around me started cheering and stomping their feet excitedly.

'I hope you're all super excited to be here today and look forward to being a part of this family for the next eight weeks! For those of you who are new and are here for the very first time, we especially welcome you. Our returners and instructors will do everything they can to help you settle in. My name is Tony and I'm one of the camp directors here along with my beautiful wife Mayamiko.'

He turned to his left of the stage and a Malawian lady walked out onto the stage wearing a puffy bright blue dress with white flowers and a matching hat. She waved out to the crowd with a big smile on her face whilst the audience continued erupting with cheers and excitement. Mayamiko took the microphone from her husband and said:

'Yes, welcome everyone today to our beautiful summer camp here in Mangochi. Our camp is very unique and special to us and we've combined both my husband's American camp traditions with our own Malawian traditions to embrace our two very different cultures. I especially hope you can find a place to store the experiences you'll face here inside your hearts and treasure us when you leave after eight weeks and continue on with your daily lives, wherever that might be. I'm sure a lot of you are still exhausted from your commutes to get here so, we won't go into anything too energy consuming just yet, but we will start our camp traditions by singing the Malawian National Anthem both in English and Chichewa. I ask you all kindly to stand up while we sing the anthem.'

Everyone stood up. Some lyrics appeared on the two screens next to the stage. Mayamiko said one last thing before the music started playing:

'Don't worry, if you don't know the words, just try to follow the tune.'

The music started playing and everyone started singing the anthem in English first.

'Oh God bless our land of Malawi, keep it a land of peace.
Put down each and every enemy, hunger, disease, envy.
Join together all our hearts as one, that we'll be free from fear.
Bless our leaders, each and every one, and Mother Malawi.'

We then sung it in Chichewa which I tried to sing along to, but the words just didn't make any sense to me. Then, we sat back down on the grass to await our next instruction.

We were guided to the dining area for dinner which was a local fish called chambo with chips and salad. It was an open space under a giant baobab tree with several picnic tables scattered about in the area. There were also long wide tables looped around the baobab tree with six Malawian ladies ready to serve the food to us. The food looked absolutely delicious and I was starving but all I could see were carbs, so I asked:

'Can I just have a plate of salad, please?'

She handed me a plate with what I requested and quickly moved onto the next camper. I found a picnic table that said "Bunk Madzi" and had a list of six names on it including my own so, I sat down. Shortly afterwards, five other girls around my age joined the picnic table. We all sat around in awkward silence for a few minutes till one of the girls who looked a bit like a tomboy said:

'Hi, I'm Amy and I'm from South Africa. Where are you

from?'

'I'm Lottie and I'm from England.'

'Nice to meet you, Lottie. We've never had someone from England here before.'

The other girls nodded in agreement.

'This is Samantha from Zimbabwe, Chabata from Zambia and Thoko and Joyce from Malawi. This is our third year here at camp except for you and Joyce who are here for the first time.'

I was relieved to find out that I wasn't the only newbie around here.

'So, what type of things do we do here at camp?' I asked.

Amy replied:

'Oh, there are loads of activities to choose from! They're broken down into various categories like Water, Nature, Arts, Sports and Leisure but there are loads within each of those categories.'

Thoko jumped in and said:

'After dinner, there's always an evening activity as well which can range from a movie night to talent shows and more which are always super cool.'

Samantha added:

'Oh, and let's not forget the excursions that happen every two weeks. I can't wait to go to Liwonde, it's one of my favourite places. Is this your first time in Malawi?'

I smiled and replied:

'Yes, my mother grew up here as a child and wanted me to experience it or something.'

'Well, there's no better place to start than being a part of Bunk Madzi,' Amy reassuringly said.

'What does "madzi" mean anyway?' I asked.

Thoko replied: 'It means "water" in Chichewa which is the local language here. As Tony and Mayamiko explained earlier, this camp is a mix of American and Malawian cultures blended together so, all of the bunks have Chichewa names.'

Tony interrupted dinner by making an announcement on the microphone.

'Good evening everyone, I hope you've managed to find your bunkmates and enjoyed those delicious chambo fillets and chips. Let's give a round of applause to the chef, Amos, and the rest of the kitchen staff please.'

Everyone started applauding and the chef lifted his chef hat to acknowledge it. Then, we turned our attention back to Tony who continued with:

'I just wanted to let you know that our first evening activity will be by the stage we were at earlier today, where we'll be having an outdoor movie night with …drum roll please.'

Everyone in the room started tapping their fingers on the picnic tables to make a drumming noise.

'Camp Rock!'

There were various reactions to this, some cheers, some grunts and some who had never heard of it.

'This movie will definitely get you into summer spirits. Enjoy the rest of your dinner.'

Once the girls and I finished eating, we got up and I followed them to the wash area. There were long and wide sinks with several taps for water to run through.

'Isn't there like a dish washer, we can put our dishes in?'

The other girls chuckled as Amy said:

'Ha try telling that to Escom. It would probably cause a

power-cut the second you put it on.'

We quietly washed our dishes and then, put them in plastic basins nearby for the kitchen staff to collect. Then, we headed out to the stage to watch Camp Rock.

After the movie, the girls and I headed to our bunk. It was a cute little wooden cabin with a small balcony. Just before the entrance, on the right, there was a big rock with the word "Madzi" painted on it and a little lantern on the left to show light at night when it got dark. We stepped inside to find all of our things already unpacked. The others weren't surprised by this, but I was quite impressed.

There was a triangle shaped platform above the bunkbeds with a small ladder to climb onto the platform which was where the bunk leader slept apparently. Then, below the risen platform, there were three wooden bunkbeds, one beside each wall of the bunk. On the right of the entrance, there was a small walk-in wardrobe with several wooden shelves with all of our clothes folded neatly on separate shelves. Then, to the left of the wardrobe, there was a bathroom that had two showers, two toilets, two washbasins and a giant mirror. All of our stuff was already arranged, so I was sharing a bunkbed with Chabata on the left. Amy and Thoko were sharing a bunkbed on the back wall. Lastly, Samantha and Joyce were sharing the right-hand side bunkbed.

A slightly older but still fairly young girl entered the bunk wearing the same uniform that Kyle was wearing earlier. She was a person of colour with black puffy hair. She had a warm smile and wore a light layer of black eyeliner around her eyes. She also had a red lanyard with her name on it. She greeted us with a big smile.

'Hello girls. I'm Emma and I'm your bunk leader this summer! I'm so excited as we're going to have some great adventures and of course, loads of fun together for the next eight weeks! Please have a seat as I have so many things to tell you all.'

Emma sat down on the floor, so we all followed suit.

'Now, I know you're all tired and just want to head to bed but we're going to do a quick ice-breaker and pick our activities for the week which we will do every Sunday. Then, I'll briefly explain the structure of the camp before we all catch up on our beauty sleep for tomorrow. So, we are going to play a game where I've invited you all to a party and you have to bring something to the party. But I've created a rule about what you can bring so, you have to figure out the rule.'

We all nodded to show we understood and then, she gestured to the girl on her left to start by saying the phrase:

'My name is… and I will bring… to the party.'

As we each went around trying to figure out the rule, I observed each of my bunkmates and discovered that you can tell a lot about a person based on what they wear.

Chabata, who I was sharing my bunkbed with was by far the fashionista. She had her black puffy hair tied up neatly with a red headband type of thing and was wearing a pair of light blue high waisted jeans and a white top with a red heart on it. We could definitely trade fashion tips with one another.

Amy had a sporty figure and kept her long blonde hair tied-up in a ponytail. Her clothes were simple as she wore a pair of black shorts with a dark green shirt with a small antelope on it along with the words that read "Springboks." Oh My Socks! She clearly has never heard of concealer as I could spot at least three pimples on her forehead!

I admired Samantha's gorgeous long ginger wavy thick hair and her little freckles on her cheeks. They say gingers always have the most fun in life. Her smile told it all.

Thoko is all about colour. She was wearing a multicoloured headscarf of some sort wrapped around her head with a matching strapless dress and blue eye shadow. The colours suited her dark skin perfectly. I made a mental note to find out what this head band trend was all about as that's clearly popular around here!

Lastly, Joyce, who had her hair in black skinny braids and was just wearing dark brown jeans and a bright red t-shirt. Oh no! She obviously needs some guidance! Red and brown are a no no when it comes to fashion.

Turns out the rule was that the item has to start with the same letter as your first name. We diverted our attention back to Emma who said:

'Brilliant! I can't wait to get to know you all better over the next eight weeks. Right, so your first three activity categories this week are Water, Nature and the Arts. Don't worry, there are loads of activities in each of those categories to choose from and you'll have the chance to mingle with other campers.'

She handed out pieces of paper with the list of activities in each category and pencils to each of us.

'All you have to do is write your name at the top and circle one of the activities in each section. Don't worry, if you're not a big fan of any of the choices as you only do it for one week and you'll have different ones to choose from next Sunday.'

I started with the Water activities which were *Fishing*, definitely not, I thought. *Snorkelling*, why would I want to look at fish? *Swimming*, seems all right and *Water-Sports*, maybe not for the first week. So, I decided to take *Swimming* as I suspected Amy would too, so I wouldn't be by myself at least.

The Nature activities included *Gardening*, too dirty I thought. *Nature-Walks*, pretty straightforward and *Photography*, not so sure I can use a camera. I circled *Nature-Walks*.

Lastly the Arts, *Dance and Storytelling*, I'm too clumsy. *Band Practise*, I can't play any instruments. *Drama*, I do love the theatre. *Sandcastle-making*, boring. *Pottery*, too sticky. *Arts and Crafts*, nope. I circled *Drama*.

When we were finished, we handed our papers back to Emma. She then explained that breakfast is at eight and that it was time for us to go to bed. She also collected all of our phones into a small box for safety reasons which I wasn't so comfortable with, but I just reassured myself that I would get it back tomorrow morning. We chimed 'Night' and got ourselves settled and ready for bed. We also had to unravel the mosquito nets hanging above the bunkbeds to reduce our chances of getting malaria which scared me a little as I drifted off to sleep.

13

First day

At 7:30am, Emma came into the bunk to wake us all up. I panicked slightly as I normally need at least an hour to get ready in the morning! I must have been exhausted from all of the travelling yesterday to have slept in that late! I was baffled by the mosquito net and tried to get past it, grabbed my essentials and dashed to the bathroom to get dressed. The other girls kept giving me, "she's crazy," looks whilst they slowly got themselves ready. Breakfast consisted of a range of cereal options, various fruits, toast and yogurt.

After breakfast, we went back to the bunk to find Emma waiting by the balcony for us to return. She smiled and said:

'Good morning girls! I hope you all slept well and enjoyed your yummy breakfast. The first day is always so hectic so, you might not see me for most of the day unfortunately. Anyway, before you disappear to your first activity, you all need to do morning chores to keep the bunk clean throughout the day. I'll be inspecting it later so, please make me proud!'

She pointed to a chart she had created and had placed next

to the entrance of the walk-in wardrobe which gave each of us an assigned cleaning task and a schedule for the week. I got assigned sweeping.

Eww, this is so not cool. I thought.

Emma looked at her watch and said:

'Right, you all know what to do now, so let's get going please! I'll be back before your first activity which is swimming!'

She dashed out of the bunk. Joyce handed me a broom which I just stared at blankly, not really sure what to do with it. The others got going with their tasks without much complaint. After a few minutes, Amy could see I still didn't know how to do my task. So, she came over and took the broom and started pushing the brush backwards and forwards to demonstrate what to do and said:

'That's what you have to do.'

We all picked swimming, which was our morning activity, so I followed the others to the swimming pool area. It was huge! There were two swimming pools, one large and deep and the other was medium and shallow. Our swimming instructor was funny enough, Kyle, who picked me up from the airport yesterday. We were the last to arrive. Kyle said:

'Bunk Madzi, you're late.'

The girls all murmured:

'Sorry, Kyle.'

Kyle then said:

'Ok, as I was explaining to the others. We'll be in the shallow pool today so; I can assess your individual swimming abilities. Those who are confident in the water will progress to the bigger swimming pool tomorrow. For now, line up with the others according to how well you think you can swim, the least confident down here to the most confident up here.'

Amy and Samantha immediately went to the top end of the swimming pool. Chabata went to the middle section. Joyce and Thoko went to the bottom end. I joined Chabata in the middle section. Kyle then said:

'Excellent! Now I know you're all cold, but you need to jump in and then we'll get all warmed up.'

We all jumped in, one at a time. There were about twenty of us so, not too crammed at least but the water made us all shiver as it was so cold.

'Very good, now you can do any stroke you like from your end of the pool to my end of the pool and back to where you are now. Go.'

Everybody started swimming like it was a race to the other side. I swam as best I could in doggy paddle but looking around, there was no way I could keep up with the others. Once we all finished demonstrating a swimming stroke, Kyle handed out floats to everyone.

'Today, we're going to work on breaststroke. So, you're going to hold both hands on the float and just practise kicking your legs like a frog, there and back. Go.'

Everyone followed Kyle's instructions. I couldn't understand why we had to swim like a frog, it seemed ridiculous, but I tried it anyway.

'Good, now this might be a little tricky for some, but you're going to put the float in between your legs and practise using your arms which is the exact same motion as you just did with your legs. Go.'

It was certainly tricky as the float kept wanting to come back up to the surface, but I seemed to be getting the hang of it.

'Very good. Now put your floats back onto the side of the pool please.'

We put them to the side.

'Now, you're going to try and swim there and back doing both the arm and leg movements at the same time. Go.'

It was a weird sensation and difficult to time my arms and legs in sync, but I'd never felt more alive in the water before I tried swimming breaststroke.

'Good job everyone, you can now have a free swim as we've finished our swimming lesson for today. Enjoy.'

Chabata turned to me and said:

'Did you enjoy that?'

'Yeah, I did actually, I don't have swimming lessons back at home, so it was nice to learn how to swim like a frog.'

We both laughed at that comment. Chabata grabbed a beach ball that was floating around and asked:

'Do you want to play catch or something?'

'Sure.'

We volleyed the ball back and forth between us for a bit. I asked:

'So, which Nature activity did you sign-up for?'

'Photography, you?'

'Nature-Walks.'

We had some time to relax in the bunk before lunch. I desperately wanted to surf the web on my phone, but Emma still kept our phones in the office. I asked Samantha when we would get them back.

'The only place in this camp that has signal is the social hut which we're only allowed to go to when we get assigned the Leisure activity.'

'Oh, but what about our parents? What if we want to talk to them?' I asked.

Samantha smiled.

'We get assigned a specific day of the week where the office arranges a phone call for us to have with each of our families. Then, when we get assigned Leisure, you can go on Facebook or whatever else you want to do. However, we won't get Leisure every week as we're supposed to embrace being in the outdoors.'

This camp was worse than I thought.

After lunch, Joyce and I joined the other Nature-Walkers at the meeting point which was just in front of the office. A young and hippie like Malawian instructor appeared, clicking his fingers as though he was jamming to a beat. He introduced himself as Luka. He had a musician feel about him.

'I'll be guiding you through your Nature-Walk today. Feel free to talk with your new friends but just be willing to absorb the beautiful nature that surrounds you. Now, follow me.'

We followed Luka to this large, rectangular shaped, red metal gate that was connected to a tall brick wall that surrounded the whole camp. I had no idea I was in such a prison. A serious looking Malawian watchman appeared out of a small little white hut that was next to the gate. Luka greeted him by giving him a high five.

'Ey, Geoffrey, how's it going man? I'm just taking these guys for a walk.'

Geoffrey smiled.

'That's cool Luka, I'll just sign you out on the form.'

He opened the gate to let us all through. We walked alongside a tarmac road and walked past a few mud huts with local families, some chickens, goats and skinny dogs. Some young children in second-hand clothes watched us with admiration and then, put their hands out begging for money. Luka must have told them to stop as they ran off. Then, Luka lead us up a mountain and warned us to be careful of slippery rocks. It was humid and there were so many annoying insects hovering around us. I kept swatting at them. Joyce was walking behind me, and I could hear her giggle with amusement. I turned around feeling annoyed.

'Sorry, do I amuse you?'

Joyce stopped her giggles and said:

'Well, they're just flies. I've never seen someone being so bothered...'

I rolled my eyes.

'Well, I don't want to catch some kind of disease out here in the wilderness!'

Joyce smirked slightly and said:

'You're just over-reacting.'

I ignored her and stayed focused on the path.

Not long afterwards, we reached the top of the mountain. The view was spectacular. You could see the blue waters of the lake shimmering in the sunlight in the distance. All the villages looked tiny as did the buildings of Camp Kulingana. There were a lot of green trees and dusty roads below. My Instagram followers would have loved to have seen this. I asked Luka:

'Excuse me sir, is there any possible way of getting a picture of this beautiful view?'

Luka smiled and said:

'Why, yes of course, you can capture an image in your mind that will bring you peace whenever you search for it.'

Seriously? Who is this guy? I was feeling very frustrated.

My fingers were consistently rubbing each other as I missed my phone more than anything right now. I stomped off to find Joyce admiring the view. I went to her for a chat.

'Where are you from again?'

Joyce explained:

'I'm from a place called Mulanje where my village is.'

I was shocked to hear that.

'Oh, I see.'

I knew then that I had nothing in common with this girl. Joyce continued to explain her story saying:

'Yeah, but I live in Lilongwe with my aunt where I go to school as my parents couldn't afford my school fees.'

I gave a reassuring smile.

'I saw a village on the bus ride to camp and it didn't look like much fun to live in. What's that like? Being poor, having no money, living in a dirty home...'

Joyce started to get annoyed.

'You know, I'm not so privileged as you! I'm only here at this camp because a sponsor was kind enough to donate enough money for me to be here as my family couldn't afford it!'

I rolled my eyes and said mockingly:

'Oh, look at me, I'm so poor and my parents can't even afford to send me to school.'

Joyce burst into tears. Everyone was observing the commotion when Luka came over to see what the fuss was about. Joyce explained the situation to Luka in Chichewa which I couldn't understand. Luka then said:

'Right, sorry everyone. We're going to have to cut this short and take these two back to camp as I'm sure Mayamiko will want to hear about this.'

'No! I swear I didn't mean to cause any harm,' I defended myself.

'Enough! We'll let Mayamiko be the judge of this.'

'Not again,' I said under my breath.

'What did you say?' Luka asked.

'Nothing,' I said.

Joyce and I sat on a bench outside the camp directors' office. Emma and Luka were arguing with Mayamiko inside. Shortly afterwards, Emma came out. She knelt down by Joyce and said:

'Joyce, I'm so sorry about what happened. I'm going to have a serious talk with Lottie about it but why don't you go and join the other Nature-Walkers? I hear Luka has a really fun game for all of you to play.'

Joyce smiled at her.

'Ok, thanks Emma.'

Emma stood up again.

'You're very welcome.'

Then, Joyce disappeared off to join the others for the rest of the activity. Emma sat down in Joyce's place and with a stern look.

'Lottie, what happened up there?'

I didn't say anything. Emma sighed.

'I've been told something along the lines of you asked Joyce, 'what's it like being poor and having no money to afford things?'

I interrupted her with:

'Can I talk to my mum, please?'

Emma looked at me with concern and said:

'Lottie, I'm trying to help you… Joyce has a very different life to yours.'

She paused.

'Which is why Tony and Mayamiko set up this sponsor scheme to allow those to enjoy what the camp has to offer when they couldn't otherwise afford it. It demonstrates equality despite all the little factors. So, please be a little bit more considerate of others' feelings in the future.'

I just kept looking at the ground avoiding eye contact. Emma stood up.

'Okay, I'll call your mother then.'

'Will I get sent home?'

Emma shook her head.

'It's standard procedure to inform parents of inappropriate behaviour. But no, you're not going to be sent home, but I do want you to apologise to Joyce for what you said.'

I looked at her.

'And if I don't want to?'

Emma sighed.

'With time, you will.'

14

Rumours

Rumours were spreading throughout the camp. Some said we had a cat fight up there on the mountain. Some changed the words from what we actually said to make them sound worse. Mealtimes were particularly bad as it felt like all eyes were on me. Even my own bunkmates were avoiding me a little. It was only the second official day of camp and I still didn't have any friends; not much different to my life in England. Kyle announced the final list of swimming groups for the week at breakfast. I got placed into the intermediate group. He must have made a mistake as I knew I wasn't that good.

Emma arranged for me to have a phone call with Mother after lunch. I was delighted as it meant I got to skip Nature-Walks, but I was also a little nervous as I knew Mother would not be happy with me. I sat outside of the camp directors' office on the bench for my phone call. Mother answered fairly quickly saying:

'Hello, this is Leslie Sheldon speaking.'

'Hi Mum. It's me, Lottie.'

'Hello sweetheart. How are you? How's the camp going?'

I tried to fight away my tears as her voice reminded me of how much I missed her.

'It's ok I guess except for the fact that everybody hates me.'

She said in a concerned voice:

'Yes, your bunk leader, Emma, called me yesterday to say you had got into some trouble with one of the girls in your bunk? Do you want to talk about it?'

The tears were getting harder to resist.

'Um… I was angry cause they took our phones away… and I tried to ask my bunkmate, Joyce, about where she was from?'

I took a breath and then continued.

'She said she's from a village and that her family is so poor that they can't even afford to send her to school. I didn't know how to relate to this girl as I don't know anything about a village. Then, she got annoyed and called me privileged.'

The tears were streaming out now.

'So, I said, 'Oh, look at me, I'm so poor that my parents can't even afford to send me to school,' but I swear I didn't mean any of it, Mum, I just don't know what I could possibly have in common with anyone here. I'm sorry.'

I could hear my mother sigh.

'Lottie, take a deep breath, you need to calm down.'

I breathed in and out a few times and then my mother continued.

'I know it's difficult Lottie, but you have only been at camp for two days! I'm sure the others are just curious about you but are feeling as though you don't want to open up to them. Do you see where I'm going with this?'

I sighed.

'Yeah, kinda.'

'Maybe you should try and find common interests through the activities? Or maybe you'll find someone who likes Ellie Nickels as much as you do? Rather than focusing on where people are from as that might be a little trickier to find common ground on.'

My tears started to fade away.

'Yeah, ok, I'll try that thanks.'

'Lottie, I imagine you feel like nobody will want to be friends with you now, but people just love to get involved with a little drama, even when they shouldn't! It'll calm down and people will move on. And perhaps you have more in common with Joyce than you think. Try to find a way to say sorry, sweetheart. But try and be a little more open to people as well as they probably just want to get to know you a little bit more.'

'Mum, I know you're trying to help... but... I swear no one will want to be friends with me... I mean why would they?'

'Just cause your friends back home disappeared when you needed their support doesn't mean you won't have friends here at camp.'

'Okay... I'll try and make amends.'

I started to smile a little again.

'I miss you a lot, Mum.'

'I miss you too Lottie, and I'm proud of you for giving the camp another go, I can't wait to hear what you get up to throughout the next eight weeks.'

'Mum, before you go, have you heard any more news about, you know?'

'Sweetheart, all you need to do is take it off your mind and just enjoy being a teenager. Can you do that for me, please?'

'Of course.'

'Good, now I'm afraid I need to go now Lottie, but I love you lots, and I'll speak to you soon.'

'Ok, bye Mum. I love you too and I'll speak to you soon.'

'Bye sweetheart.'

I still had an hour till Drama, so I went back to the bunk to relax for a bit till then. I found some printed photos of Nicole, Emily and I and I decided to stick them on the wall by my bed. There was a photo of me and Emily doing silly poses from this Eighties theme day we had at our school recently. It made me laugh, that was such a good day. Then, there was a photo of all three of us posed by Nicole's swimming pool with our feet dipped in. There was a sudden cold pit in my stomach as I traced my mind back to… *The girls and I were standing outside the biology classroom. Robbie approached us with his hands in his pockets trying to look cool. He smiled as our eyes locked with one another.*

'Hey… um… Lottie, could I speak to you about something?'

'Hey Robbie, of course. Excuse me girls.'

I placed a hand on his arm.

'What would you like to ask me?'

He touched his hair momentarily, cleared his throat.

'I was wondering if you wanted to go to the party with me later?'

'Yes, that sounds good to me.'

I twirled my ponytail as he continued saying.

'Why don't we exchange numbers and I'll text you later on, yeah?'

I slipped my hand into his trouser pockets, pulled out his phone and handed it to him for his pin code. He entered it and then I typed my number in.

'Shall we meet at four?' I asked.

'Works for me. See ya later, yeah?'

'See ya.'

He walked away as I turned to the girls beaming with excitement.

'Oh My Socks! I can't believe Robbie actually asked me out!'

Emily smiled whereas Nicole frowned.

'Aren't you happy for me, Nicole?'

'I am but...'

Emily interrupted her.

'Of course, we are girl! Now you better get yourself to biology and don't forget to update us at the party, yeah?'

'Yeah, of course, right see you gals later.'

'See ya.'

I walked off to biology but just as I was about to enter the class, I glanced at the girls to find Emily comforting Nicole about something. She was probably just anxious about her birthday party I thought as I entered biology.

'Lottie? Are you in the bunk?'

I sat up on my bed.

'I'm right here, Emma.'

'Oh good. Just letting you know that it's time for Drama.'

'Thanks Emma, I'll head over there just now.'

I quickly grabbed the photos and tore them into pieces and threw them into the bin before dashing out for Drama. Mother said I needed to switch my mind off from... the photos needed to go.

15

Loyalty

Back in England, Nicole and I were clothes shopping when she asked:

'I wonder what the camp is like that Lottie's at?'

'Who cares? She probably has to hide away from mosquitos and has to sleep in a mud hut so how could that be any fun?' I replied.

'Well, we can't know that and besides, at least she's having an adventure whereas the most exciting thing that's happening here are the summer sales.'

'Nicole, I thought we were tired of Lottie constantly ditching us every time a boy shows interest in her?'

'I mean it is annoying, but she did help out with the party invites and at least she came to my birthday party... That's already an improvement compared to other times.'

'You mean the party invites *I found* whereas she just changed the colours?'

'Oh yeah, that's true.'

I walked off to the jeans section and then Nicole followed

saying:

'Em, I'm sorry I didn't give you more credit for the invitations. They were really cool.'

'Thanks, Nicole. Can I ask you something?'

'Of course.'

'What would you do if a friend framed another friend for something really bad that they didn't actually do?'

'Which friend is this?'

I gulped.

'Er... Rosie... She got Claire into detention for... cheating on a maths test when actually she did it.'

'Well, if you or Lottie did that to me, I would be quite disappointed because that's not what friends do... especially best friends.'

It was like I had just pooped my pants as I asked:

'Yeah, but what if Claire wasn't that great at being Rosie's best friend?'

'Well, perhaps Rosie should have spoken to Claire about whatever she was doing that upset her because Claire doesn't deserve to go to detention for something that Rosie did in spite of their friendship.'

'Yeah, you're right but maybe Rosie felt as though Claire wouldn't listen to what she had to say.'

'Well, then I guess they're just not meant to be best friends then.'

I hung up the clothes I had selected back onto the railings near me and said:

'Hey, I need to go home... I think I'm coming down with a migraine.'

'Oh no, do you want me to come with you?'

'No, don't be silly. You've found so many great clothes. I'll be fine.'

'Ok, I'll text you later then to check in with you.'

'Thanks, I appreciate that. Bye!'

I dashed out of the store as fast as I could and then, spent the rest of the walk to Oxford Street tube station with tears flooding out of my eyes as I realised how incredibly stupid I was for framing Lottie for Robbie's murder. How could I possibly fix this?

16

The boy who was late

I was surprised to see that breakfast consisted of bacon, eggs and sausages. I was sure I wouldn't have had a chance to have an English breakfast till I returned back to England. It was a nice reminder of home at least. Was it still my home? I was starting to get a hang of sweeping the bunk till our cleaning tasks got changed for the new week. I was now assigned: making the beds.

How hard could it be? If I could manage sweeping for a week then I could definitely make the beds. I was in need of a fresh start.

I was the only one who chose Volleyball from my bunk. The other girls chose Horse-riding, Basketball or Tennis. Volleyball took place on the sandy beach that looked out onto the blue wavy waters of the lake. I recognised some of the others from previous activities but didn't know any of their names. A very energetic and happy Malawian girl approached me with a massive smile on her face. She had short wavy black hair and was missing both of her front teeth. She was shorter than me and wore a pair of black shorts with a plain green t-shirt and worn-out trainers. She introduced herself:

'Hi, I'm Chichi. I noticed you were by yourself and was wondering if you wanted to be my friend?'

'Yes, that's very nice of you, thank you. I'm Lottie.'

She grinned.

'Oh, I know who you are. Lottie Sheldon from England, right? I heard you got into a misunderstanding with some other girl last week.'

This seemed to happen to me a lot lately, but I calmly said: 'Yup, that's me.'

'Hey, don't worry about it. People were just curious about you as you're the first we've ever had from England.'

A loud whistle blew followed by a young athletic looking instructor. She kept her brunette hair tied-up in a ponytail. She spoke confidently with an American accent.

'Sorry I'm late. I got caught up in a staff meeting. My name is Nicky and I'll be your volleyball instructor this week. Right, hands up if you've played volleyball before?'

Several hands went up.

'Hands up if you've played competitively before?'

A few hands went up.

'Ok, what I want you to do is to get into pairs and practice volleying to each other. I'll come around and help those who are struggling or don't know how to volley.'

Chichi and I grabbed a volleyball and practised volleying to each other. Nicky came around and seemed to be happy with our technique. Then, we went on a short jog around the volleyball area and did some stretches to get warmed up. The session was mainly about different passing and receiving techniques followed by a few games of volleyball. Chichi and I definitely had team chemistry as we just seemed unstoppable. It was a lot of fun. It looked like I had made my first official friend here at camp.

Later that day, my bunkmates and I walked to the social hut together. I was so excited to update my Instagram followers. However, just when I was about to post an update, the wi-fi cut off. Another power cut. What was I supposed to do now? Chichi found me and asked:

'Why the sad face?'

I sighed.

'I was just really looking forward to catching up on Instagram.'

Chichi grinned.

'Ah, don't worry about it. Come play bao with me instead.'

'Bow? What's that?'

'It's this really cool game, you'll like it, come on.'

Bao was a game I'd never heard of back in England. There was a long wooden board with four rows of eight holes filled with stones. Each player had two rows each and the objective was to clear a whole row of the opponent's side of the board. You clear their side by "stealing" their stones and your turn ends when you only have one stone left in a hole. Chichi was an amazing player but I soon caught up and got the hang of it for myself. We happily passed the time playing Bao that I almost forgot to get ready for Water-Sports.

There were three speed boats, each with their own Water-Sport option: tubing, banana boat and wakeboarding/water skiing. Suddenly, I spotted this super cute boy running along the sandy beach towards the speed boats. He had a slightly tanned and athletic body, brown pushed-back hair, hazel brown eyes, pearly white teeth and a smile that would make you melt in an instant. I could feel butterflies circulating in my tummy. Henry, the instructor followed my gaze and said:

'Bryan, you're late.'

He apologised.

'Sorry sir, I lost track of time.'

Bryan looked over in my direction, gave me a massive smile and winked at me. I blushed and shyly looked at the ground. Only six people were allowed in each boat. I noticed Bryan chose wakeboarding. So, I did too.

I sat next to this girl on the speed boat who had blonde hair tied-up together in a ponytail and wore braces on her teeth. I was already disgusted by her. Henry explained that we would start with water-skiing as it would be easier to wakeboard after we got the hang of the basics. Then, we were each given a life jacket for safety reasons and off we went to a deeper section of the lake. I could feel my hair blowing from the speed of the boat. There were a few smaller islands in the distance, but we stopped right in the middle of this massive lake.

Bryan was very eager to go first but because he was late, Henry chose me instead. I was quite nervous as I'd never done anything like this before, but Henry reassured me that I'll be fine. I jumped into the water, feeling refreshed from the baking sun. Then, Henry passed the water-skis to me to slip onto my feet. He handed me a rope that was connected to the boat and slowly started backing the speed boat away from me. I lay there with these skis sticking out of the water and the rope in between my legs. I reminded myself of the advice we received earlier which was to use the rope to lift yourself gently out of the water. He gave me a thumbs up to see if I was ready. I gave him one back. However, as the speed boat slowly picked up some more speed. I wasn't quite expecting it and let go of the rope without much success. The speed boat came back a few minutes later, I was so sure Henry would laugh at me but instead he said:

'Don't worry, most first timers react like that but I'm confident you'll get it this time.'

I replied:

'Ok, I'll try again.'

This time, I managed to lift myself up with the rope. I could feel my hair blowing in the wind as a rush of adrenaline creeped inside of me whilst letting the skis guide me along the water. It felt incredible. I had the biggest smile on my face. Then, I hit a wave and face plummeted to the water. It stung a bit, but I was fine. The speed boat returned. The girl with the braces jumped into the water. So, I slipped out of the water skis to pass them onto her. Then, I swam around the back of the boat to climb up a small ladder to get back onto the boat. Bryan handed me a blue towel. He gazed into my eyes with a big smile on his face.

'Nice one, Lottie.'

He actually knew my name!

'Thanks!'

We spent the first hour each having a turn on the water-skis before we moved onto wakeboarding. Henry explained that it's slightly harder as you have to turn yourself ninety degrees immediately after you get up from the water. We went in the same order as before which meant I was the first to try it. I jumped back into the cold water with my life jacket securely on. Then, Henry handed me the wakeboard so I could strap my feet in, similar to a snowboard. I received the rope and the boat slowly drifted away from me. It was a lot harder than water skiing as you have to actually pull yourself up rather than just let the water guide you up. Then, maintain your balance as you turn ninety degrees to the right. It felt insanely more thrilling though. A few minutes later, the boat turned which I wasn't quite prepared for and fell backwards. As I rose back up to the surface, I beamed with pride that I managed to do it first time without fail. Henry was impressed as he said:

'That was quite a step up from last time, Lottie, well done!'

It was the first time in a while where I felt confident about something. I also couldn't help but wonder if Bryan was impressed enough with my performance.

17

The African bush

It was time for our first weekend excursion which was Liwonde National Park. I overheard my bunkmates talking about it whilst they were packing their sleepover bag. They were excited about the night drive and seeing all of their favourite animals again. I stopped packing and panicked as I realised where we were actually going.

'Wait, are you telling me, we're going to a safari park?'

They all looked puzzled and said:

'Yes, it is literally the best excursion on the list!'

'But what if we get attacked or something?' I asked.

All of the girls laughed except for Joyce. Samantha said:

'Relax ok? They know how to protect us; we won't get attacked.'

I wasn't so sure about that.

The bus ride took an hour and half to get to Liwonde National Park. I sat back in my seat, plugged my headphones in and glanced out the window. It was a nice sunny day just like when... *I was standing outside the library holding Nicole's party*

invitations. A group of boys from the year above were approaching
including Robbie. I had the biggest crush in the world on him, but
I didn't exist in his world. They walked past me and entered the
library all except for Robbie who took the invitation I was holding
out in my hand and he said:

'Thanks.'

'You're welcome.'

Those were my first words ever to Robbie as he caught up with
his mates.

Would he actually come to the party? I secretly hoped he would.

What I thought was the safari park turned out to be a wide and long brownish river surrounded by various bushes and trees with shades of browns and greens. A speedy silver well maintained speedboat came towards the riverbank we had stationed the bus at to collect us and took us over to the campsite. I could hear some hippos chuckle in the distance. I felt nervous as I entered the speedboat; Chichi gave my knee a little squeeze and a smile to indicate that we were safe. Wilfred, the guide, gave us a safety brief on staying in the speedboat at all times, no dipping our hands into the crocodile and hippo infested river and to not make any loud noises if we happen to pass any of the animals. Trust me, I was definitely staying put, there was no doubt about that. Once we were ready, the speedboat slowly reversed out and glided softly across the river to the opposite side where these giant tents started slowly appearing from the blurry distance.

We finally arrived at Mvuu Camp and were greeted by other Malawians ready to welcome us and help us with our bags. They offered some apple or orange juice for us to drink. We walked up the pebble stoned path to a giant complex where the dining area, bar and reception were located. There were many chairs and sofas for us to sit on. I spotted a few boa boards which I was certain Chichi would be up for a game or two later. There were no windows. Instead, the walls were high enough to prevent a fall but were low enough to look out onto the river below. There were also a few statues of hippos scattered about as well as crocodile skulls for decoration. We sat down by the chairs while our instructors discussed the room arrangements. We were then taken to our chalets.

The chalet was like a giant tent with a thatched roof above it. There were two rooms, one as you entered that had a double bed presented with mosquito nets hanging above. The other was round the back with six single beds spaced out evenly. Each bed had a small welcome note and a miniature wooden hippo sculpture for us to keep. That was a cute gesture. There was a small bathroom as well. Our guide explained that we should keep the door locked at all times and that there was a siren available only for emergency situations such as an animal entering our chalet. However, he reassured us that it has rarely ever happened.

Our night drive started at 3:30pm where we jumped into these dark green safari jeeps with Wilfred again as our guide for the evening. We had another safety brief like before and then set off to see what animals we could find. We soon came across a herd of impala; a group of bright orange deer who scurried off in fear of us preying on them. Wilfred stopped the jeep and explained an interesting fact about impalas which was that they have four chambers inside their stomachs and basically eat till they fill up all four chambers which is why they're constantly seen eating. There were also some baboons picking on some fruits from a tree and a couple of warthogs knelt down munching on a patch of grass. We continued driving along this vast open landscape of short grasses and trees both standing by proudly and fallen because of damage by elephants. About ten minutes later, we came across a herd of cautious looking waterbuck who looked like brown reindeer with big ears sticking out and a carefully circulated white ring on their bottoms.

'It is believed that the ring around their bottoms is because one day, they sat on a toilet seat with wet paint on it,' Wilfred explained. We chuckled with amusement at the idea of that.

The alpha male led the herd away from the jeep with their twenty or more followers following single file behind him. We then drove along a small bridge to get past a ditch but stopped to have a look at a trail of mongoose footprints printed delicately in the mud. Wilfred explained that the best way to track down the animals is through the trails they leave behind. As the sun was coming down, we stopped by the river. Wilfred stepped out of the jeep and went around the back to take out the cool box that had a range of soft drinks and snacks for us. Everyone started climbing out of the jeep, I couldn't believe my eyes.

What were they thinking? Did they want to get killed?

Those were the thoughts on my mind. Chabata came to my side of the jeep and asked:

'Lottie, are you ok?'

'Yeah, I'm fine thanks. I just don't understand why everyone has got out of the jeep, when we're still out in the bush?'

'Oh, that's cause we're having sundowners! It's where we watch the sunset, it's really beautiful and the National Park ranger at the front has a gun if any animals do decide to attack us.'

'Really? Oh ok, I still feel safer in the jeep to be honest.'

'The animals won't attack us unless they feel we're attacking them, and they basically see the jeep as a predator anyway. You should come down, the sunset will happen in seconds and you'll have a better view down here, I promise.'

'Hhmm I don't know Chabata...'

'Come on Lottie, didn't your parents send you here for an adventure?'

'Yeah, that's true I guess... Okay, I'll come down but I'm still a little scared.'

'Don't worry, stick with me and I'll fight any lions that come our way.'

She put up her fists like she was a boxer. It made me laugh.

'Haha I doubt you'd have much of a chance to be honest but thanks.'

'That's what friends are for.'

Chabata was right, this really was worth seeing even if I couldn't help but watch over my shoulder every thirty seconds. The animals grew quieter as everything around us turned pitch black except for the sun that burst into a giant yellow ball and spread orange and red rays across the sky as though it had to make a dramatic exit before signing off for the day. We lifted our bottles of coca-cola and sprite into the air and cheered for a great summer ahead. Then, once the sun completely disappeared, we jumped back into the jeep back towards the camp. The National Park ranger sat right at the front of the vehicle with some kind of torch thing, he was called the 'spotter,' as he would help us find the smallest of animals out here as we sat in total darkness. As we drove along with the spotter flashing the torch left, right, up and down in the trees and on the ground, I still had no idea how he found this, but we stopped by a giant tree where a small little bush baby was snuggled on a tree branch. It looked a bit like a bat crossed over with a lemur with its big eyes reflecting the torch rays. After a few minutes, we continued on passing by some more impala which we didn't stop for as we were focused on finding the animals we don't usually see during the day. Some mongoose scurried across from one bush to another. Then suddenly, we came across an elephant limping on its own.

It had stepped on a nail that had punctured his foot. It was heart-breaking to watch. The spotter lowered the torch to avoid disturbing the elephant. Wilfred stopped the car. He put his finger up by his lips towards us to emphasise being quiet. The elephant noticed us and turned to face us. He watched us very carefully. Then, he started gesturing a run-up movement with his limping foot, as well as grunting in frustration, ready to charge at us. I was terrified. I wanted to scream with terror. Amy noticed this and covered my mouth with her hand, whilst calmly reassuring me, that it was going to be ok. The elephant eventually gave up and continued on his way. I took deep breaths just trying to process my near-death experience.

Dinner was a barbecue of various meats with rice or potatoes next to a campfire. I sat next to Chichi for dinner and we compared our safari drive experiences with one another as we were both in different jeeps. She didn't get to see any elephants, but she did see some zebras which I would have loved to have seen.

'Well, they are wild. They're not tamed like zoo animals,' Chichi said.

After dinner, a guide with a gun walked us back to our chalets for our safety where we settled down to sleep for the night.

It must have been about two in the morning when I woke up to grunting noises outside our chalet. I grabbed a torch that was underneath my bed and flashed it towards the sound. The tent reflected a shadow of a hippo chewing grass nearby.

Surely this was considered an emergency, right?

I went over to Emma's bed and shook her awake. Emma very sleepily said:

'Hmm what is it Lottie?'

I nervously said:

'I think there's a hippo outside the chalet.'

Emma reassured me with:

'It's ok Lottie, it won't hurt us.'

Then, she turned over and went back to sleep. I crept back to bed and tried to sleep again but kept waking up to any new noises I heard from outside.

Emma woke us all up at 4:30am to give us enough time to get ready for the morning bush walk. We all moaned about getting up so early, but Emma enthusiastically said it would be worth it. Wilfred met us by the jeeps with a giant walking stick and the spotter from last night holding his gun. He once again gave us a safety brief putting emphasis on us walking in single file in complete silence as to not disturb the animals and for our own safety as well. The skies revealed patches of reds and blues not quite ready to reveal the sun just yet whilst the birds were all chirping frantically hidden in the trees. Wilfred stopped us and asked:

'Does anyone know why the birds are making so much

noise?'

Chichi answered:

'Is it because they've spotted a lion or something to warn the others?'

Wilfred replied:

'Not quite, they're announcing that they survived the night as they are most vulnerable at night. If they don't hear a response from their partner, then they also announce they are single and looking for a new mate as well.'

We set off towards the bush where the sun was slowly starting to reappear for the start of a new day with impala and baboons taking the opportunity to eat their breakfast. There were various trails of mongoose, impala and even rhinos as we walked along. It was like solving a murder mystery that occurred while we slept in our chalets, though there were no traces of any kills nearby. We came across a weird looking tree that looked like a snake had wrapped itself around it when it was actually a plant called Python Vine. Wilfred explained that the plant needs a host to survive without causing any harm to the host. We continued walking through various bushes, pushing branches out of our way until we came across a pile of dung and a curvy animal body print in the sand. Wilfred stopped us once again and asked if anyone recognised the animal that had laid there during the night. Amy said:

'I think it's a hippo.'

Wilfred said:

'That's correct but how did you know?'

Amy answered:

'You can kind of tell from the shape at the front and the back end of this print.'

Wilfred was delighted to have had such a good student as he said:

'Well done young lady, you're absolutely correct. Now when you think about it, it's a bit like the hippo made a home here with this pile of dung being the bathroom and his bed right here where the print has been left.'

We all gave a chuckle at that concept. The time for the walk was coming to an end, so, we started walking back towards the camp which wasn't that far ahead of us. Wilfred received a radio call and stopped to respond. He got excited as he announced:

'There's been cheetah spotted! If anyone wants to see them, we can quickly jump into a jeep and try and find them. They're a very rare sighting here in Liwonde.'

We all agreed with excitement as we walked quickly back towards the camp. We jumped into the jeep and off we went like a wolf hunting down its prey. We managed to find the other jeep that had spotted the cheetah. Wilfred stopped the jeep right next to it as we quietly watched this beautiful cheetah lying down on the ground, ready for a nap, without any interest in us whatsoever. It was by far the biggest highlight of the weekend.

I was actually quite sad about heading back to Camp Kulingana as there was something about the African bush that just made me want to stay longer. All my friends chimed that it was an excuse for me to come back next year. It was starting to get harder and harder to hate Camp Kulingana as it felt more like home than England did.

18

Betrayal

The following morning, Emma walked beside me on our way to the dining area for breakfast. She asked:

'Lottie, how are you finding the camp? Do you think you're settling down a bit more?'

'Yeah, I think I'm starting to like this place a little bit more. Chichi is my main friend but others are warming up to me. I quite enjoy the activities but still not the greatest fan of the food to be honest.'

Emma smiled.

'Oh good! I'm very glad to hear that, Lottie. I also see you've signed up for some different activities than usual this week which I hope you'll keep doing.'

She gave my shoulder a quick squeeze and headed towards the director's office.

Chabata and I both had Photography, so we walked together to the activity. She noticed that I was smiling and out of curiosity asked:

'Hhmm, don't think I've actually seen you smile since you've arrived here. What's changed?'

I blushed.

'Not sure really, just starting to warm up to this place.'

Chabata smiled. There was a table with all sorts of cameras waiting to be picked up. Chabata picked up two and gave me one of them and said:

'You'll need a camera to do Photography.'

I laughed and looked into the camera lens to get a feel of it. Bryan was on the other side making a silly face into the camera.

'Hey, haven't seen you for a while. How are you?'

Bryan smiled which sent a tingle to my knees.

'Wow, that actually worked haha. Yeah, I'm good thanks, how about yourself?'

'I'm quite all right, thank you.'

He grinned and said:

'I had no idea you were so posh.'

'Yeah, I'm from England so…'

'That's cool, I'm from Zimbabwe.'

'Oh, cool.'

Bryan scratched his head and asked:

'Um… Do you want to be partners for this? I mean if there happens to be partner work… I don't know for sure.'

'Sure, I'll certainly be your partner, if we do any partner work,' I smiled.

'Cool, thanks.'

Our Photography task was to capture movement on the camera. There were various stations set up with things we could use and in pairs, we helped each other create the movements we wanted to capture. Bryan and I went to a station with a small baby pool filled with water and tennis balls. We took turns bouncing the tennis balls into the baby pool whilst the other tried to capture it. At least that's what we were meant to do. Instead, we started a water-fight with one another till our clothes got soaked. We still managed to take a few pictures, so our instructor wasn't that annoyed about it. After the session, Bryan walked me back to my bunk.

'Well, that was some crazy fun, right?' Bryan asked.

I blushed.

'Yeah, it was, just as well we have some time to get changed.'

'Will you sit with me at lunch?' he asked.

'Sure, see you then,' I said with the biggest smile on my face.

'See you.'

He gave a little wave and jogged off to his own bunk.

I wasn't sure if this counted as a first date or not. I was a little nervous but excited as well. It reminded me of.... *I found Robbie waiting just outside of Cookie Crush for me. He was wearing black jeans and a white button-up shirt with black Ray-Ban sunglasses.*

'Hey, you're looking good tonight,' he said.

'Hey, why thank you. You're quite dressed up for an ice cream date?'

'Well, I thought we were going to Nicole's party after?'

'Of course, we are.'

Once we ordered our ice creams and sat in a booth. We exchanged our biggest secrets with one another and his was:

'League of Legends mostly... I've actually got tickets to go watch the professionals play next month which I'm very excited for.'

You would have loved watching those professionals play, Robbie. I'm so sorry you weren't able to. I looked up at the bunk ceiling as though I was talking to his spirit and wiped away a tear as I entered the bathroom to get changed.

Not long afterwards at lunch, we were eating pizza slices when I asked:

'So, do you have any siblings?'

'Yeah, got a younger brother called Harry whose also at this Camp. What about you?' he said.

'I'm an only child.'

'Oh lucky. You must get loads of cool stuff.'

'Yeah, I guess I do. We live in quite a nice part of London and we have a lady who comes in every day to clean. But my dad travels a lot for business trips, so I don't get to see him that much.'

'That's a shame. I also live in a big house and I have a maid and a gardener, don't know what you think of that?' he grinned.

'Haha, I didn't realise we have such similar lifestyles,' I said followed by a smile.

'I've been to London before as I have cousins... Sorry, a cousin who lives there... I wouldn't say it's a similar lifestyle haha,' he said.

'That's fair... So, does everyone live in a big house here?' I asked.

'I can't know for sure but if they can afford to go to Camp Kulingana for eight weeks then yes, they probably do.'

'And everyone has a maid?'

'It depends, we consider it more as providing jobs for the locals rather than an expression of wealth,' he said.

'Oh, I see. One of my bunkmates said she came from a village and was here through a sponsorship. I just didn't know how to relate to that and assumed maybe everyone here lived in like a mud hut or something?' My cheeks flushed with embarrassment.

'Haha, I suppose you think we know how to defend ourselves against a lion or something as well?' he asked.

'Do you?'

'No, sorry! Anyway, yes, we do have some campers from poorer backgrounds here. They usually only get to come here for one summer which is a bummer.'

We noticed other campers were starting to clean-up and head to their next activities. Bryan asked:

'What are your next activities?'

'Um... Drama and Tennis. What about you?' I asked.

'Damn, Band Practise and then Football. I'll see you at dinner then?'

'Ok, can't wait.' I said with a smile.

Bryan smiled back as we headed to the sinks to clean-up our dishes.

That evening, there was the long-awaited disco night. The girls and I were all getting ready in the bunk. Amy was helping Samantha straighten her wavy hair while Chabata and Thoko did each other's makeup. Joyce was looking into a mirror, holding up two dresses, trying to decide what to wear so, I decided to help her.

'The red dress,' I said.

Joyce turned around and said:

'You think so?'

'It'll be perfect,' I said with a smile.

'Thanks.'

She went to the bathroom to put it on. When she came out, I helped her zip-up her dress at the back. I hesitated slightly as I said:

'Hey, Joyce?'

She turned around to give me her full attention as I continued saying.

'I'm sorry about how I acted that day when you were telling me about where you were from. It's just that when you said you came from a village, I felt it was impossible for me to relate to you as I have such a different life back in England and it just all came out wrong. Can we be friends again?'

Joyce smiled and said:

'Yeah, I'm also sorry Lottie. I suppose I was just a little jealous of you as everyone was constantly talking about you and your life sounds so much better than mine. And of course, we can be friends again.'

'It's not that great to be honest.'

Joyce and I hugged each other. Then, she asked:

'Now, who is this boy you keep sneaking off to be with at mealtimes?'

I blushed.

'Oh, he's this boy I met at Water-Sports last week and his name is Bryan.'

'Well, do you know what you'll be wearing tonight?'

I grabbed this plain strapless blue dress that reached my knees to show Joyce.

She smiled and said:

'That'll look perfect.'

Amy suggested that we should create a big entrance to capture everyone's attention at the disco. As we approached the sportshall where the disco was taking place, the song, 'Spotlight' by DJ Mike was playing. We all posed by the entrance and then tossed our hair to our right-shoulders like a wave once the second verse started. It worked perfectly and we all felt like celebrities. Then, we ran to the dancefloor for the song, 'Drop it' by HB. Where we dropped down to the floor just like the lyrics instructed to do so. 'Love me' by ZiZi followed and then, 'It's time to party,' by Lying Kings.

I noticed Chabata had disappeared somewhere. I also had yet to see Bryan anywhere. I asked Chichi to come help me find him. We went to the drinks and snacks table first partly because we were thirsty, but we also thought he might be there getting a drink as well. He was not.

Then, we tried looking out onto the dancefloor, but we still couldn't find him. So, we went outside to cool down from the sweat to find Bryan leaning by a tree towards another girl who I identified as Chabata. We watched them closely. They kept whispering things to one another. My heart was pounding with fury. I wasn't sure what was going to happen. Chabata appeared to be quite flirty towards him, trying to hold hands with him or laugh at things he'd said. I couldn't tell if Bryan liked her or not, but he definitely liked the attention. Then, Chabata stood up and my heart sunk as she kissed him.

I tried to fight back my tears as I didn't want to create a scene and dragged Chichi back inside with me. 'Superheroes' by Smithy was playing, and everyone began doing a particular dance choreography especially when the chorus was on, acting like a superhero. Chichi kept trying to get my attention to see if I was ok. The truth is that I was not. I couldn't understand why I was reacting like this. I mean, it's not like he was my boyfriend or anything. It's just, nothing made any sense and my heart felt like it wanted to burst into flames. I tried to use the music and dancing as a distraction, but I suddenly recalled flashes of *people drinking alcohol from red plastic cups;* I felt like throwing-up and my head was spinning, so I decided to get a drink to cool down and process my thoughts a little bit. The music just wasn't enough to distract me. There, I found a boy who looked quite similar to Bryan. He had an athletic body, dark brown eyes, fairly long brown hair with a fringe that flicked over to his left side. He caught my eye and walked over to me. He asked:

'Hey, are you having fun?'

'No, not really.'

I took another sip of my juice. The boy kept gazing into my eyes and said:

'Aww, well, the night's not over and you're definitely the most beautiful girl in this room.'

I smiled.

'Thanks.'

I put my hand out to shake his hand.

'I'm Lottie, by the way.'

He shook my hand and said:

'Josh. May I have a dance with the prettiest girl in the room?'

He then kissed my hand. How could I possibly say no? I mean, here's a boy that actually wanted me. There was conveniently a slow song playing in the background while Josh guided me to the dancefloor for a slow dance. I put my arms around his neck and stared into his dark brown eyes. My mind kept replaying the kiss I had just witnessed, and Josh could tell something was up as he asked.

'Now, what's made you so sad this evening?'

I sighed:

'I'll never get a boyfriend.'

I looked down to the ground.

Josh said:

'Hey, look at me.'

I moved my gaze towards his eyes. Then, he said:

'I think I know what might help.'

He pursed his lips onto mine and kissed me. It brought back the sparks I felt when… *Robbie and I arrived at Nicole's house but just before we entered, he said:*

'Lottie, I'm having so much fun with you tonight, I think you're incredible.'

'Oh, thanks Robbie, I'm having a lot of fun with you too.'

He leaned down towards me, took hold of my head in his gentle hands and pursed his lips onto mine where it felt all tingly and mushy. After a few minutes, he pulled away, pushed a few loose strands of my golden curly locks over my shoulder and then took hold of my hand again as we entered the house.

I pulled back from Josh and said:

'That's just made things worse.'

And walked away from him.

19

Hidden secrets

At Photography, Bryan kept trying to get my attention. He would make silly faces at me or try and poke me. I ignored him and even deliberately paired with someone new. I wasn't ready to confront him about the kiss. At lunch, he passed by our table and said:

'Hey Lottie, what happened at Photography earlier? I thought we were a team?'

'Felt like I needed a new partner in crime.'

He left the table. Why was he still chasing me when he clearly likes Chabata? I wondered.

He'd be better off without me anyway; I would just end up hurting him.

That night, I had a dream where I recalled… Finding Robbie lying dead next to me.

'Who did this to you?' I shouted at the top of my lungs.

'The attic,' his ghostly figure replied.

'What do you mean?' I asked.

I felt a hand shake my body and opened my eyes to find

Chabata staring at me.

'Bad dream?' She whispered.

'What do you want?' I said as I turned over to my side.

'Lottie, I need to show you something.'

I crept out of bed as quietly as I could. Chabata looked at me and said:

'You might want to put on a jumper and leggings or jeans or something.'

'Why?' I asked.

'Because it's cold outside and we have to be quick before the others wake up, especially Emma.'

I slipped on some black leggings and a college jumper using the torch that Chabata handed to me. Then, we sneaked out of the bunk. Once we were out of earshot of the others. I asked:

'Chabata, where are we going?'

'Shh… you'll see,' she said.

We walked to the sandy beach where I could see a flicker of a campfire and I could hear some laughter. I turned to Chabata and said:

'Wait, I don't understand. What's going on?'

'Bryan asked me to bring you here, but you have to swear you won't tell anyone about this. Ok?'

'Wait… Bryan asked you to bring me here?'

'Yeah, he did… A bunch of us sneak out sometimes and just chill for a couple of hours on the beach and then, we head back to the bunks before any instructors find out we've been out during the night. So, just be cool, ok?'

Other than Bryan and Chabata, I didn't recognise any of the other faces around the fire. Some were smoking, some were drinking beer and others were just chatting. The smell of the beer made my stomach groan. I caught Bryan's eye and he nodded for me to follow him.

'Hey,' I said.

'Hey, why are you avoiding me?'

'I saw you and Chabata together at the disco last night.'

'Oh.'

He clearly wasn't expecting that.

'Did you kiss her?'

'What? No… I mean… It didn't mean anything.'

'What?'

Bryan sighed:

'Lottie, trust me when I say that it didn't mean anything… I was a little nervous about something and Chabata helped me out.'

He was hiding something as far as I could tell. I turned and started walking away. Bryan started to panic and said:

'I've never kissed a girl before.'

I turned around to face him whilst he tried to explain himself again.

'I've never kissed a girl before and I was scared I would mess it up or something. Chabata and I are good friends from previous camp years and she just helped me get my nerves out of my system. I never meant for it to hurt you; it was more like homework to get it right for when I'd get the chance to kiss you.'

Those butterflies found their way back into my stomach. Bryan took hold of my hands and looked deeply into my eyes and said:

'I solemnly swear that you're the only girl here that I want to kiss.'

'Bryan…'

'I swear, Lottie.'

He leaned towards my lips, but I interrupted him with:

'There's something you should know about me.'

'Ok… What is it?'

'We should sit down.'

We lowered ourselves and sat comfortably on the sandy and cold beach.

'I'm not quite sure how to tell you this… A couple of months ago before I came here… there was a party, and I went on a date with a boy from my school… my therapist said I have some condition that prevents me from recalling the events of that night… due to the trauma… but one thing I do know is that… the boy I was on a date with… was found dead the following morning…'

He interrupted me and asked:

'What was the name of this boy?'

'Robbie Wilson.'

He stood up onto his two feet and backed away from me.

'You mean to tell me, that you're the one who killed my cousin?'

I gasped.

'Robbie, is your COUSIN?'

'Yes, he is… he's from my mother's side of the family.'

'Bryan… please… let me explain…'

'You've said all I needed to hear, thanks.'

He ran off towards the bunks and I slowly headed towards the same direction. I suspected he would report me to the directors tomorrow morning, and I would be sent home. The whole point of me being at this camp was to get away from all things associated with Robbie's death but instead, it followed me here... But he deserved to know the real me.

20

I need your help

I walked up to the caravan that Chip lived in and knocked on the door. He opened it and with a fag in his mouth said:

'All right babe, I was wondering when I'd next see you.'

He gestured for me to enter and so, I did and then, I said:

'Chip, we have to tell the police.'

'What are you talking about?'

'You know what I'm talking about…It's our fault, not Lottie's.'

'Why are you dragging me into this? It was your idea, not mine!'

'No. You were the one who suggested we frame Lottie!'

'Actually, what I recall is that I suggested we dispose of the body including your little friend… But you didn't want to do that.'

'She doesn't deserve this, Chip… Please, I need your help.'

'Oh yeah? Let me ask you this: who do you want to go to jail? Huh? Because I was the one who brought in the drugs and the judge won't look twice at my innocence. Especially with my dad already in jail.'

'Of course, I don't want you to go to jail.'

'Well, then stick to the plan… I'm sure your "friend" has fancy lawyers or whatever that will bail her out or reduce her sentence anyway.'

'I just feel awful and helpless in this situation.'

He lay on his bed and tapped it.

'I did say you owed me. Maybe I'll make you feel a little bit better too.'

I lay next to him and let him kiss and touch me. I felt like a mannequin but at least it distracted me from the mess I had got myself into.

21

The long bus ride

A few days had passed, and we were preparing for our next excursion to Luwawa Forest Lodge.

'Survival skills?' I asked.

'Yes, the fourth week of camp is a bit different, as the excursion is a whole week rather than just a weekend, to give you all a valuable opportunity to learn skills you'll likely need throughout your life!' Emma explained enthusiastically.

I had never experienced being lost in the wilderness before and as I looked around the room, I felt anxious that the others may be more experienced at this.

It was about a six-hour drive from Camp Kulingana. We left at six in the morning in order to arrive in the afternoon. I decided to sit next to Chichi for the bus ride as they put all the girls on one bus and then the boys on the other. It would have been an opportunity to confront Bryan, but I was certain there would be other opportunities during the excursion to do so.

'So, have you talked to Bryan at all since the disco?' Chichi asked.

I promised I wouldn't tell anyone about the "sneak out," and this definitely wouldn't be a good time to mention it either with instructors nearby.

'Yeah, I have. Apparently, he's never kissed a girl before and was super nervous and so, Chabata offered to help him get his nerves out of the way for when he'd get the chance to kiss me. It was super sweet when you think about it.'

'But has he kissed you yet?'

'No, not yet.'

'I think he's lying, Lottie. You know what boys are like? They lie all the time to make you believe what they want you to believe.'

'Well, I can't know for sure, but I trust him.'

I took out my iPhone.

'Do you want to listen to some music with me?' I asked.

'Sure, what do you like to listen to?'

'Mostly pop. My favourite singer is Ellie Nickels at the moment.'

'Never heard of her but yeah, why not?'

I handed her one of my earbuds whilst I inserted the other in my ear and clicked on the shuffle button. Chichi took out some paper and a pen and we started playing hangman to pass the time. About every two hours, we stopped at a small petrol station in case anyone needed the toilet or just wanted to stretch about given it was such a long journey. About eleven, Emma and the other instructor, Mary, started handing out bottles of water, crisps and sandwiches for everyone to eat for lunch. Then at about two, we finally arrived at Luwawa Forest Lodge.

The owner of Luwawa Forest Lodge came out to greet us.

He introduced himself as Chris Swan. He had cropped brown boyish hair and brown eyes. He was quite tall and had an authoritative air about him. He wore a white shirt with the lodge's logo on it which was a blue hummingbird flying over a forest. He also wore dark grey shorts and big chunky brown hiking boots. We followed him into the dining area. It looked very cosy as there were a few sofas to sit on, a fireplace and a baobab tree painted on the wall with the sun rising in the background. Chris explained the general plan of the week which consisted of learning some basic survival skills, long walks and a survival test to put our newly acquired skills into action. For now, we had the rest of the day off to relax after that long bus ride we had.

We got shown to our rooms which were two small bricked cottages. One for the girls and the other for the boys. Each cottage had two floors. The top floor had several bunkbeds for us to sleep in. The bottom floor consisted of a small kitchen, a living room with a tv and a small dining area. We weren't using the kitchen during our stay though as they had kitchen staff who could accommodate our numbers. We were told that we could relax and do whatever we fancied as long as we didn't leave the lodge area.

Chichi and I started walking towards the field near the dining area as we'd overheard the other girls talking about the boys having a football match. Bryan stopped us and said:

'Hey Lottie! Can we talk?'

'Hey Bryan... um... I'm kinda busy right now so maybe later?'

'Busy doing what?'

'We're heading to the field to watch the football match some of the boys are playing.'

That was by far the lamest excuse I could come up with. I just wasn't ready to answer his questions about Robbie as I barely knew the answers myself.

22

Survival 101

The next morning, we entered the dining room to find a range of cereals, toast, jams, fruits and some fresh juices for breakfast. We had a big day ahead of us, so we were advised to eat well for the activities ahead as they were energy consuming.

'Good morning everyone!'

Chris sounded very upbeat and excited.

'I hope you all slept well and enjoyed your afternoon of relaxation yesterday. From now on, it's all about survival skills! Meet us just out front after breakfast with your learning caps on.'

Chris asked us all to line up according to our birthdays from the youngest to the oldest then, he assigned everyone a number from one to four. I got given a two along with Bryan, a boy called Josh, an Indian girl called Mishka and a blonde-haired boy called Sam. Mishka had shoulder length black hair, hazel brown eyes and came across as a natural leader. Sam had blonde hair, an awkward shaped mouth with big pursed lips and blue eyes.

I kept looking at Josh because he looked familiar until I

finally realised that he was the boy I kissed at the disco. Oh My Socks! I haven't even told Bryan yet about that!

We were taken to an area with four concrete blocks, four wooden planks and two car tires. Each team squeezed onto one of the blocks and waited for further instruction. Chris explained that the objective was to simply get your team from one block to another block but there were certain conditions.

1. One team member was "blind" and would have to wear a blindfold.

Mishka volunteered for our group.

2. One member had a "broken leg" and would have to hop on one leg.

Bryan said he was happy to do it.

3. One team member would not be allowed to speak at all which I volunteered to do.

4. If any of us fell off at any point whilst trying to get to another block then, that person would be "eaten by crocodiles."

5. The team who got the most people to another block would win a prize.

Josh suggested we throw the tire in the middle of the two blocks and have someone jump onto the tire to help connect the two wooden planks together for everyone to get across. No one objected, so we decided to try it and the team on the other side agreed as well.

Sam helped Josh throw the tire successfully in the middle. Then, Josh stretched his legs out as far as he could until he touched the tire. He nearly lost his balance but somehow managed to get himself onto the tire. Then, Sam passed a plank to Josh and they both secured it so we could all cross onto the tire. The other team did the same. Now, it was time to test if our plan would work. We chose Mishka who was "blind" to go first. I helped guide Mishka towards the plank whilst Sam held onto the plank to secure it and then Josh was ready to receive her. She walked very slowly as she was unable to see where she was going but we successfully managed to get her to the other side despite anticipating her falling to the ground. Then, we did the same for the other group's "blind" person. We decided Bryan would go next as he needed more help, given he had a "broken leg." Sam and I both put a foot on the plank to secure it whilst helping guide Bryan onto the plank. It was going smoothly until Bryan got to Josh, he lost his balance and dragged Josh with him as they both fell onto the ground which meant they were out. Their fall also meant we lost our two planks, and we didn't have any other resources to get us safely to the tire in the middle, so our two teams got disqualified from the competition. We were all a bit disappointed that the strategy didn't work but kept our heads high for the next activity.

After a quick ten-minute break, we did the classic human knot exercise where everyone grabs onto two different hands in a circle and then you have to try and find a way to unknot yourselves. It was such a silly exercise and yet, some of the knots were really complex to unravel. We were then given an hour to relax before lunch. Chichi and I decided to use the time to play go fish with some cards we found in the cottage.

'Is everything okay with you and Bryan?' She asked.

'Yeah, why do you ask?'

'It just seemed like you were avoiding him yesterday.'

'I was just feeling tired from the long bus ride.'

Another lie.

After lunch, Chris explained that our generation rely way too much on Google maps to get us from A to B but when you're lost in the wilderness with no signal, you have to come up with an alternative method. Each group was given a compass and a map of the lodge area. We were taught how to use a compass and discussed as a group other methods as well. One suggested paying close attention to any nearby sounds you hear. Then, we were taught basic skills such as setting up shelter, purifying water and catching and killing prey to eat. By the time dinner came around, I was starving. Bryan had asked me to meet him at the playground after dinner which I agreed to as I knew I couldn't avoid him forever.

After dinner, I walked to the playground and sat on the swings. Bryan came shortly afterwards and did the same. Some of the others would do a wolf call as they walked by to tease us. But once it was quiet. I said:

'I was surprised you didn't report me as a murderer.'

'I wanted to… But I figured you wouldn't be here at camp if you truly were a murderer. In some ways, I haven't fully processed his death.'

'How can you be so sure that I'm not?'

'I remember you mentioned something about a therapist?'

'Yeah, she felt this camp would help me recover from the trauma of it all and yet, I can't stop thinking about it… I even have nightmares about it.'

'Does anyone else know?'

'No… I probably shouldn't have told you, but I just felt that I should… You deserve to know the real me.'

'Your secret is safe with me.'

'Thanks, I appreciate that.'

'I do like you, Lottie… a lot actually… it's just a bit complicated… this Robbie thing I mean.'

'I understand… Do you want to tell me more about him?'

'Not tonight… But I will. Now, come here for a second.'

I got up from my swing seat and gave Bryan a hug who was still sitting on his swing seat.

As I pulled away from our embrace, he leaned closer towards me and kissed me and this time, I let him as I wanted to kiss him too. Just five minutes without Robbie haunting my mind was the best thing I could ask for.

23

A night in the forest

After two intense days of learning essential survival skills, it was finally time for the survival test!

We were all very curious to see what this adventure would be. Each group received a giant bottle of drinking water, a compass, a map, a tent, a torch, a walkie-talkie and a box of matches. Then, we all followed Chris on a trail to the starting point. Shortly afterwards, we arrived in a wide green trimmed field. Chris handed out an envelope to all of the groups and explained:

'The envelope contains the first clue to solve. One of your instructors or one of our forest guides will be stationed at each of the check points displayed on your map.'

We all looked at our maps which had six red crosses scattered about that represented the check points.

'The first group to successfully arrive back at the lodge with all five wristbands, which you'll collect from each check point wins.'

That certainly got everyone talking until Chris mentioned:

'I have to warn you though that in the past, some groups have taken several days to arrive back. Please don't panic as we have provided some items to help you survive if need be and the walkie-talkie can also be used to contact us. There will also be a car driving every three hours along the route of the map to check your progress. If your group has not come back by Saturday, we will send a search party to come look for you. Please stay in your groups. Good luck and I hope you manage to effectively use the skills we've taught you all during the past couple of days as well as enjoy this adventure we've created for you all. Good luck!'

I opened the envelope and read it out loud to the rest of my group. It read:

'*Navigate your group to a source of water and catch a fish.*'

Josh grinned and said:

'That's so easy. We'll definitely return to the lodge by tonight.'

'Maybe they're starting off easy and gradually making it harder as we go along?' I suggested.

Bryan took out the map from my hand and pointed out a giant lake on it. Everyone started cheering and giving each other high fives except for Mishka. She cleverly pointed out:

'We still have to get ourselves to the lake before we can celebrate. As well as use a compass.'

Sam placed the compass in his hand and then turned the dial to the east. The map indicated that direction and then, he slowly turned himself till the red arrow was pointed in the direction we wanted to walk in. We walked through a forest with tall green and rusty pine trees. There were various fern bushes below the trees as well as several insects lurking about. The best part of the walk was holding hands with Bryan, the tingles reminded me of the kiss we had shared. Sam was right as ten minutes later; we found a giant glistening lake shimmering in the sun. The lake was surrounded by hundreds of pine trees and bushes. The water itself wasn't exactly a Mediterranean blue but we were very happy to have found it anyway. The sun was scorching hot and as a group, we decided we didn't want to waste the drinking water we had. There were a few rumbling stomachs set off in the group so, we decided to stop for lunch.

Josh pulled out a pocketknife from his pocket, picked up a fallen branch and started carving a spear out of it. Bryan and Sam worked on setting a campfire for us to cook the fish. Mishka was foraging for things to eat with the fish while I untangled an old fishing net I found near the lake. Using the fishing net and Josh's carved spear, we managed to catch three big juicy fishes to eat. We all cheered with excitement.

After lunch, we walked along the edges of the lake and soon came across a giant tent with the Luwawa Lodge symbol on it. There was a Malawian man there who ticked our names off the list and handed us a woven bracelet with a small "one" on it as well as an envelope with the next task. It read:

'*Navigate your group to a forest. Set up a campsite and spend a night there. Someone will come in the morning to award you your bracelet.*'

Mishka began to panic.

'No! I refuse to spend a night in that forest! What if we get attacked or something?'

None of us were particularly thrilled about the quest until I said:

'Look Mishka. You won't be on your own, we'll all stay together as a group which will make it more fun. Josh has a pocketknife that we can use, and the boys know how to make a fire and I honestly don't think they would ask us to do this if we were in any serious danger. If anything, it's probably just to scare us a little.'

We ventured deep into the forest away from the lake. We found some dry ground and pulled out the tent, pegs and the instructions on how to set it up. As I read through the instructions, I came across something important.

'Guys.'

Everyone paused what they were doing to listen.

'The instructions say it's a two-person tent.'

Mishka burst out in frustration.

'Great! So, three of us will catch hypothermia or something all to save two people? I knew this was going to be a bad idea!'

'Woah, calm down, Mishka! We'll figure something out,' I said.

'Oh yeah? Like what?'

Bryan suggested:

'We can try and build some kind of shelter? It won't be as pleasant as this tent but it's only one night, so it wouldn't be the worst thing.'

I smiled.

'That's a great idea, Bryan!'

'Thanks, Lottie.'

Josh on the other hand wasn't quite on board as he said:

'And who will have the privilege to sleep in the tent? I think Bryan just wants to use this as an excuse to spend quality time with his new girlfriend!'

I felt embarrassed as the others chimed 'Ohhh' till Bryan butted in:

116

'Woah man. She's not my girlfriend and even if she was, I was not thinking that so, just shut up!'

I was confused.

'Wait, I'm not your girlfriend? But you kissed me the other night, did that not mean anything to you?'

Bryan blushed.

'No, Lottie, that's not what I meant.'

'Not the first time I've heard you say that.'

Josh smirked.

'Oohh, maybe you're just not good enough for her, Bryan.'

Bryan was about to throw his fist at Josh when Mishka yelled: 'STOP IT!'

They lowered their fists as she continued.

'This is exactly what they're testing us on! Remember what Chris said yesterday? When you find yourself in a survival situation, you have to learn to trust each other and work together as a group.'

We put aside our differences to listen to her plan.

'Let's focus on building the rest of this campsite and then, we can decide later who sleeps in the tent because I don't know what time it is, but I don't want to try and build this up when it gets dark.'

The plan was to gather up fallen branches to lean against a nearby tree and leaves for the floor. It wasn't the best alternative, but it was the only kind of shelter we could think of. Then, Bryan and Sam set up a fire again while Josh created a snare to catch any rabbits that might be lurking by for dinner. Mishka and I finished putting the tent together. The sun was starting to set but our campsite was more or less complete. Now, we had to decide who would sleep where for the night. We agreed to create a rotation system, so everyone had some time in the tent. We gathered around the fire and ate the rabbit that Josh managed to catch. There wasn't a lot of meat on the rabbit itself which still left us all with rumbling stomachs. We shared a few stories and campfire songs to distract ourselves from feelings of hunger. Mishka had filled the drinking flask with water from the lake which we used to put the fire out. Bryan and I had the first shift with the tent. None of us had a watch and we weren't allowed our phones, so we just had to make a rough estimate of every two hours to switch places. To be honest, I'm not sure the tent was any more comfortable than the shelter we built as we didn't have any sleeping bags or blankets or pillows to use. Bryan and I lay in the tent, he tried to kiss me again, but I dodged it and said:

'You can't just kiss me again after what you said earlier tonight.'

Bryan sighed.

'Well, you're technically not my girlfriend just because I kissed you the other day.'

'I know that but… it just came across like you were disgusted by the idea of it.'

'No, of course I'm not. It just annoys me when guys bring up sex like it doesn't mean anything. Josh has a reputation around here with the girls, but I swear Lottie, I'm not like that. I just want to get to know you more and not rush into labels, if that's ok with you of course?'

'Yeah ok, that's fair. I'm sorry, I've never had a boyfriend, so I guess I'm just a little new to all of this.'

'That's ok, Lottie, and I'm sorry about what happened earlier, I just got caught up in the moment and all the words came out wrong.'

I moved closer to Bryan for a cuddle.

'You're forgiven.'

He smiled and then, we tried to get some sleep.

That night, my mind took me back to the party... *Whilst he was getting the drinks, I searched the crowd till I spotted Nicole and Emily talking to two rough looking boys I didn't recognise from school. They were both wearing white tracksuits and were hovering around the girls like they found prey to pounce on. Nicole fortunately spotted me and gestured Emily to come and greet me. At least it got them both away from those boys.*

'Happy Birthday, Nicole! The party looks great and I love what you've done to your hair!'

'Thanks, Lottie! How was your date?'

'It's been really great thanks; Robbie is just getting us drinks.'

Her hair... Oh My Socks! I missed the Glitter Chic's appointment and that's why Nicole was upset in the science corridor!

I woke up dripping with sweat and breathing short quick breaths. Bryan must have woken up too as he asked:

'Lottie, are you, all right?'

'Glitter Chic's!'

'What? What are you talking about?'

'Nicole had arranged an appointment for us to get our hair and makeup done before her birthday party, but I got so distracted by Robbie that I agreed to go on a date with him instead!'

'And?'

'That's why they were acting so weird around me... It's

because they were upset that I forgot about the Glitter Chic's appointment.'

My breathing was slowly returning to a normal pace. Before Bryan and I could talk more, a dark shadow opened the zipper of the tent and poked their head in.

'Hey guys, sorry to disturb but since you're both awake, would you mind switching places now?'

It was Mishka.

'Oh yes, of course.'

We scurried out of the tent and joined Josh by the alternative shelter whilst Sam and Mishka entered the tent. Josh lifted his eyebrows and asked:

'What was the commotion about?'

'Nothing for you to be concerned about,' Bryan hissed.

'Enough.'

I put an end to it before another fistfight could occur.

As we sat there in silence for a few minutes, I suddenly remembered that Bryan still didn't know about the kiss I had shared with Josh at the disco. Was this the right time to mention it?

A truck with men cheering some words in a language I couldn't understand suddenly emerged. They had a paraffin lamp in the back of their truck where they sat. They stopped at our campsite. My heart started beating fast as I heard one say:

'Ey, rook boys. We missed a palty here on our rand.'

I was terrified they'd notice the tent as I wasn't sure how they'd react. One of the men took some firewood out of their truck to start a new campfire. I whispered to Bryan:

'What should we do? They'll definitely notice the tent or worse us once they light the fire.'

'I don't know, we have to try and scare them somehow.'

They lit the firewood with matches, and I noticed that they were drinking from a bottle that looked similar to vodka. I pointed it out to Bryan and Josh.

'Oh My Socks! They're drinking alcohol which means they're probably drunk!'

Just as I had feared, one of them said:

'Ey, Maxwell, rook there's something ova there.'

They noticed the tent. Josh whispered:

'I've got an idea. When you hear my signal, try and get Mishka and Sam out of the tent. I'll do my best to keep them distracted.'

'But wait…' I replied.

It was too late; Josh quietly ran off while Bryan and I squeezed each other's hands for comfort. A few minutes later, we heard a wolf howl. I felt like I was about to have a heart attack, but Bryan calmly said:

'That must be the signal. Let's go.'

We carefully watched the men's reactions. It seemed to work as one said:

'Ey, what's dat sound? Are dare hyenas about?'

They all listened again and when they heard the howl again.

'I don't know but rets get out of here.'

They left the fire and drunkenly hurried back to their truck.

Meanwhile, Bryan and I rushed to open the tent.

'Mishka! Sam! Wake up! We need to get out of here now!' I said urgently.

'What? What's going on?' Mishka responded.

'There's no time, we need to move!'

We ran out of the forest as fast as we could until we eventually felt water beneath us which made us realise, we'd found the lake again. Then I pointed out.

'Where's Josh? He's still in the forest, isn't he? What if those men caught him?'

Bryan heroically said:

'You guys stay here. I'll go back and find him, but I'll need the torch.'

'No Bryan! What if something happens to you too?'

'We can't just leave him behind, we're a team, remember? Here, you guys stay here by this tree, if anyone comes, try and stay hidden. We'll be back when the sun rises.'

He grabbed the torch from me and ran back into the forest before I could change his mind. Sam, Maria and I sat down by the tree as I filled them in on what had happened.

Would we ever see them again? I feared we wouldn't.

24

Lost and found

The blazing hot sun rose and dazzled our eyes. I rubbed them hoping I'd just had a bad dream but found myself at the tree where Bryan left us last night. I was annoyed at myself for falling asleep but was concerned to find that neither of the two boys had returned. I woke up the others and we decided to try and relocate our campsite thinking maybe we'd find the boys there.

When we arrived at the campsite, we found my bunk leader Emma, there in a distressed state. I ran straight to her and hugged her. She said:

'Oh Lottie! I'm so glad to see you all, what happened?'

'Bryan and Josh are missing... There were these drunk men, and we created a distraction to scare them off but lost Josh in the process and Bryan went back to find him, but neither of them have returned... We were hoping to find them here.'

Emma took a breath and then explained:

'Chris informed us of these men that go drinking in the forest but there's been no trace of them for weeks, so Chris had hoped they wouldn't appear for the survival test. Regardless, I'm deeply sorry you all had to face that. I'll still grant you your bracelet but let's try and find the boys first.'

We found some shoe prints and decided to try and follow them hoping it would lead us to the boys. An hour later, Emma decided that we needed more help. So, she called Chris and explained the situation. He told her he'd meet us in the forest with his big green jeep. We waited at the campsite until Chris appeared in his jeep filled with snacks, bottles of water and blankets for us. We were absolutely starving as we hadn't had any breakfast.

'I think it's best if you all stay here in case they happen to return while I scout the area,' he said.

'No, I should go with you as I was there… I know what happened… I just want to help.' I offered.

Chris looked to Emma who gave him a nod and so, it was settled that I would join him with the search. We drove up and down the forest whilst I called out their names which made me anxious. Please don't be dead. I kept on repeat in my mind. I was starting to lose all hope when I heard something.

'Turn the engine off now!'

Chris obeyed. It was quiet until…

'Help!!!!'

Chris decided it might be easier to trace them on foot so, we got out of the jeep. He grabbed two torches for us, and we headed in the direction of the cries for help. Someone was running towards us, we stopped to discover it was Bryan with grazes all over his arms and forehead. I tried to hug him, but he gently pushed me away.

'Bryan, what happened to you? Are you ok? Where's Josh?'

'There's no time to explain. Josh is in danger, follow me.'

Bryan led us to a cliff by the edge of the forest. Josh had fallen into a ditch below; he wasn't able to move. My shoulders hunched up with fright at the shock of finding him in that state. Bryan placed a hand on my back to comfort me. Chris grabbed his walkie-talkie and made a radio call.

'Calling George… Calling George.'

'George speaking.'

'The boys have been found.'

Another green jeep arrived with an emergency first aid kit. Chris and two Malawian men worked together to lift Josh out of the ditch. They used a rope that had a swing looking cloth on it to lower one of the men down. He then carefully placed Josh onto the rope swing thing. Then, Chris and the other Malawian man pulled the rope swing up whilst the Malawian man below kept his hands underneath Josh to keep him steady. Once Josh reached the top, they carried Josh into the back seat of the jeep where he lay on the seats. He cradled his body in pain as they gave him some water and one of the snack boxes to restore his energy. Then, they used the rope swing to help the other Malawian man out of the ditch. The two Malawian men then drove the jeep back to the lodge while Chris, Bryan and I walked to the other jeep we had left not too far away in the forest. On our way to the jeep, I asked Bryan:

'So, what happened exactly?'

'The drunken men somehow detected the wolf thing was a prank and so they chased him… deep into the forest… but as it was so dark, he couldn't see much and… accidentally fell into the ditch… and I guess the drunken men decided to just leave him there.'

He seemed nervous; it wasn't like him.

'But… How did you manage to find him?'

'It wasn't easy… I initially went back to the campsite and realised he wasn't there… So, I began walking further trying to call out his name to see if he'd respond… I found a burning fire and thought maybe it was another group and maybe they'd seen or heard something… But then as I got closer, I saw these men wearing really scary masks and dancing around like… They were worshiping a God or something… I was so scared of them that I ran away as far as I possibly could but then… I collapsed from exhaustion and fell asleep… When the sun rose, I woke up and found myself looking at the view of the cliff… I tried to figure out where I was with my surroundings and then I heard some grunting noises… I initially thought it was an animal of some sort but… It turned out to be Josh in a ditch… I tried to get him out but… There wasn't much I could do given how badly injured he was so… I tried to comfort him and shouted out for help every now and then, just hoping someone would hear us and help out… till you both appeared.'

'Wow, that's a lot to process… I'm just glad we found you both.'

'Me too.'

When we arrived at what we thought was the spot where we had left the jeep, it had disappeared. Chris frustratedly swore.

'Shit.'

As he kicked one of the tree trunks nearby. I said:

'What do you think happened to the jeep?'

'Sorry, it's very common to have thieves lurking by around here, so they must have stolen the jeep.'

Bryan said:

'Well, what do we do now?'

'I'll radio in for another jeep to come and pick us all up.'

When we finally arrived back at the lodge. Josh was lying in a bed in the cottage in excruciating pain. He couldn't walk and kept clutching his body in more pain. Chris turned to Emma and said:

'It's very likely Josh has broken some bones from the fall but we don't have access to a hospital close by.'

Emma calmly said:

'Ok, thanks Chris. I'll call head office back at Camp Kulingana to discuss what to do next.'

Whilst Emma made the call. We all went to the dining area to have some dinner but I just couldn't face eating, so I headed to the cottage to catch up on my sleep.

The following morning, Emma explained that they decided to end the survival test given what had happened. I was disappointed but understood their reasoning. Chris was out all day trying to track down the other groups. Josh was in bed and couldn't move but we were allowed to go in and visit him. I was also very curious about:

'Hey Josh, when did you learn how to do a wolf howl?'

'Oh, my dad and I go hunting a lot and I guess it just became a hobby of mine to replicate animal sounds. Never thought it would actually be useful one day.'

'It was really impressive, it made me think there was a real wolf out there!'

'Haha, well it was the only idea I had at the time but didn't think they would come chasing after me!'

I noticed Bryan standing by the doorway observing us but when I got up to go talk to him, he disappeared. What was that about? I wondered.

Early next morning, a driver from camp arrived to take Josh to hospital. Meanwhile, the groups slowly started to reappear. I found Chichi and immediately filled her in on what had happened. She explained that her group had some difficulty as well but nothing like what we had.

After dinner, Chris gathered our attention to give an end of trip speech.

'Good evening everyone. As most of you are aware, we were forced to end the survival test earlier than expected due to unforeseen circumstances that resulted in a camper being severely injured. The main point of the survival test was to teach you all very useful survival skills and I was very proud to hear of what all the teams achieved. Please don't be discouraged by this sudden end and I really hope you've enjoyed your time here at Luwawa and the rest of the summer goes just as well and maybe I'll see some of you again next year.'

We all cheered and thanked Chris for the exciting week we'd just experienced. Then we were told to go and pack our bags and get a good night of sleep as we would be leaving early back to Camp Kulingana and we all knew how long that journey was. That night, as I lay in my bed, I kept thinking about my friends back in England...

'Oh, I almost forgot! I got all three of us makeup and hair appointments at Glitter Chic's straight after school just before the party starts,' Nicole said.

'Oh My Socks! It takes ages to secure an appointment there!'

I was the worst friend in the world to have missed that appointment but equally, why didn't the girls just remind me of the appointment instead of letting me go on a date with Robbie? Something just wasn't right.

25

Telling the truth

Nicole and I were tanning in Hyde Park and scouting for cute boys when our phones chimed with a notification.

'Hey, did you see Lottie's email?' Nicole asked.

'No, what did she say?'

'Here, I'll read it to you…'

Hey girls!

I just wanted to say that I'm so so sorry that I missed that Glitter Chic's appointment just before your birthday party, Nicole. I had completely forgotten about it until just the other day when I was thinking about your curly hair at the party. I know that makes me the worst friend in the world but thought I should at least apologise.

I can't wait to catch up with you both when I'm back from camp, I have so much to tell you about this place… It's way cooler than I imagined it would be.

Hope you're having a good summer!

L x

'That's so nice of her, don't you think? She's never apologised for anything before she went to that camp.'

I shrugged my shoulders.

'Words don't mean much. We have to see what she's like in person when she's back.'

'Em, I have to ask you something… What did you mean by 'leave it with me,' that day in the science corridor?'

I stood up and walked towards the pond that was nearby to look at the ducks in the hopes that Nicole would forget what she just asked me until:

'Em? I asked you a question?'

I took my sunglasses off and put them on my head and said:

'Do you remember that boy who brought alcohol to the party and was the leader of the party in the attic?'

'Oh yeah, Chip, wasn't it?'

'He's my boyfriend.'

'What? You kept that quiet!'

'I know… It's just I knew you and Lottie would never approve of him nor my parents, but I can't help it, he makes me feel special.'

'Really, Em?'

'Yeah, he does. Anyway, I asked for his help and he brought the cocaine we had up in the attic and the alcohol for Robbie to use…'

'Wait, was Robbie a drug addict?'

'Not exactly. He might have done some drugs before at other parties cause Chip seemed to know he would be interested in it, but I don't know…'

'Why was Chip trying to get him to take the drugs then?'

'It was stupid really, but I thought the drugs might make

him do something stupid and embarrassing... That way, Lottie would realise how pathetic he was and would be our best friend again.'

Nicole stormed off but I ran to catch up to her and said:

'Wait, Nicole! Where are you going?'

She stopped in her tracks.

'You mean to tell me that YOU killed Robbie with the drugs your so called "boyfriend" brought to MY party in MY house!'

'It was an accident, Nicole. I never meant for him to die.'

'Then, why tell the police that Lottie was responsible for his death?'

'He was already dead... Then...'

She interrupted with:

'What do you mean he was already dead?'

'When he went to the bathroom, he died whilst throwing-up, I don't know why but Lottie, Chip and I found him like that and then... Chip hit Lottie with an empty glass bottle and she passed out.'

'How did they end up in the living room then?'

'Chip wanted to dispose both of their bodies, but I didn't want to do that, so we moved their bodies to the living room... That's why we asked everyone to leave and I trapped you in the attic...'

She interrupted again.

'It was YOU who closed the attic door on us? Do you have any idea how claustrophobic I got up there?'

'I know, I'm sorry! I just didn't want you to come down and find us with the bodies and so, Chip and I put your dad's hunting dagger into Robbie's chest and put a spilled cup of alcohol near Lottie to make it look like she killed him while she was drunk.'

'I can't believe you would do this to our best friend. What kind of friend does that make you?'

'I did it for us, Nicole.'

'No. You did it for yourself because you didn't want to go to jail and I guess you wanted to protect your boyfriend too!'

'Nicole, please… I've tried to fix this, I even spoke to Chip about it.'

'And?'

'He asked me who I preferred going to jail… Him or Lottie?'

'Are you hearing yourself right now?'

'Well, he's right though that Lottie has lawyers and rich parents to get her out… Chip has nothing Nicole! You don't know him like I do.'

'Don't call me or text me again until my best friend, Emily Greene, is back because she would never frame Lottie in order to protect a boy! You're just as bad as her if you think a boy is worth saving over your own best friend!'

Then, she walked off. I walked back to the pond and sat down on a bench nearby and watched the ducks and swans as I contemplated what to do next with my life. I kept looking at my wrists and then, turning them over and then back to look at them. I took my phone out of my pocket and Google searched the helpline I was looking for that I found on Childline. Then I dialled the number, and someone responded:

'Hello, this is Michelle speaking. How may I help you today?'

I shed a few tears as I said:

'Hi, my name is Emily and I've been having suicide thoughts.'

'Before you say any more, I'm proud of you for taking the step to call us and just know that I'm here to listen to you no matter what you want to say, and I will do my best to help you move forward as suicide is not the answer to your problem.'

I took a deep breath.

'It all started when…'

26

Space

I found Bryan sitting on one of the sofas in the social hut. He looked up and smiled when he saw me. I sat next to him and said:

'Hey, did you hear about Josh?'

'Hey, yeah I did… Shame, he had to leave camp early.'

'Do you think there was anything we could have done differently that night?'

'Lottie… You don't need to blame yourself for this.'

'I guess… I just can't help but feel like I'm cursed somehow.'

'Is this because of Robbie?'

'Maybe.'

'Do you want to talk about it?'

He intertwined his hands into mine.

'Yeah… But not here.'

We got up and wandered outside to a tree that was out of hearing distance of the others.

'What was your cousin like? I didn't have many opportunities to talk to him before…'

'Robbie was great! He wasn't just a cousin to me… He was like a best friend too, he introduced me to this game called League of Legends that's…'

I interrupted him with:

'Oh yeah! He told me about that! He was meant to see the professionals play…'

'Yeah… He was actually meant to come here this summer… I was so excited to show him something cool about my world but too late for that now.'

I put a hand on Bryan's shoulder.

'I really am sorry about Robbie… I'm trying to recall as much as I can about that night, but I haven't remembered anything significant yet.'

'What about that night in the tent?'

'That night, I realised why my friends were avoiding me… I forgot about the hair and make-up appointment my best friend, Nicole, arranged for us before her birthday party started.'

'And?'

'Well, maybe it's a girl thing but we take hair and make-up seriously… I was just so excited to go on a date with your cousin… Sorry, I know that must sound weird.'

'It's alright… Do you miss your friends?'

'I do but it's a bit complicated as well.'

'Was there anything strange about that night that you can remember?'

'There were these two boys that I didn't recognise from my school… I don't know, I got an uncomfortable vibe from them.'

'Might be worth informing the investigators? You never know what might come out from it.'

'Yeah, I have been meaning to talk to my lawyer about it…

Mother too, actually.'

'That's fair.'

'There is something I kinda wanted to talk to you about though.'

'Oh, what's up?'

I blushed a little.

'I've been thinking about that night in the forest... and how terrified I was of potentially losing you forever... I really like you, a lot, Bryan, and I wanted to ask if you would like to be my boyfriend?'

Bryan hesitated for a second and then said:

'Uh... Listen, Lottie, I think you're an incredible girl and I've really enjoyed our moments together but...'

'But what?'

'I think I'm still in shock about the forest incident and the Robbie thing and just need some time to process it all, you know? I'm sorry.'

I couldn't sit and listen to any more of this, so I got up and walked back into the social hut to find Chichi by the boa boards. She could tell I was upset and asked:

'Lottie, what's wrong?'

I shrugged.

'I asked Bryan, if he wanted to be my boyfriend and he said no.'

'Oh Lottie, I'm so sorry!'

She gave me a hug and said:

'Eish..I knew he was trouble that one.'

I sighed.

'Can we just focus on the boa game?'

'Sure.'

Chichi had spent ages trying to convince me to try the Snorkelling and Gardening activities so, I decided to give them a go as I knew it wouldn't be Bryan's thing.

For Snorkelling, we got taken to a small island by a speed boat which you could see from the sandy beaches of the camp. There were only six of us in the activity including Chichi and Joyce. We put our snorkelling masks on and jumped into the water. Henry passed us two flippers each to slip onto our feet. Then, Chichi, Joyce and I dunked our heads in the water and started jetting off around the various rocks. We could see lots of small fishes of various shades of blue and yellow. Some had small little black stripes and others had scattered little specs of dots. I could see why Chichi liked snorkelling so much. It was like escaping to another world. After about forty minutes, we were starting to get a bit tired of looking at fish, so Henry suggested some rocks where it was safe to jump off from. We handed our flippers and masks back to Henry who was lounging on the speed boat and swam towards this very large rock with bird poop lining the edges of it. Once we got to the top, it felt like we ruled the world. Joyce became very nervous, but I turned to her and said:

'Joyce, this camp was meant to provide you a lifetime of experiences that you may never have again. This is one of them.'

She nervously said:

'You're right but I'm scared.'

Chichi and I grabbed her hands and in unison said:

'We'll jump together.'

We moved closer to the edges. Then, we did a count down.

'3...2...1'

Then, we leaped off whilst screaming our lungs out. It was

such a thrilling experience to crash into the blue waters of the lake. When we rose back to the surface, we were all laughing and exclaiming how cool it was and decided to try it again.

We got back to camp with half an hour to spare before our next activity which gave us plenty of time to dry off and change out of our wet swimsuits. There was as usual a power-cut, so I wasn't able to dry my hair with my hairdryer, so I just used my towel instead and then twisted it into a bun to prevent it dripping onto my clothes.

Chichi was outside my bunk waiting for me so we could walk to Gardening together. On our way there, she praised the instructor.

'Adamson is by far my favourite instructor here, he's a true expert on plants I swear.'

When we got to the gardening shed. We changed out of our shoes into wellington boots and slipped on gardening gloves. Adamson greeted us very warmly and explained we had a very exciting project to work on that day. They had just built a new fishpond and our task was to make it look pretty and present- able for the camp. It sounded like hard work to me which I wasn't a huge fan of.

The first stage involved us spreading fresh new soil around the area of the pond. I felt a bit squeamish whenever I saw a worm amongst the soil bags but Chichi kept me motivated with her passion for the project. Once the soil had been spread all over, we then had to lay these small white pebbles around the edges to make it more presentable. Then, we got onto the fun part of planting various plants around the pond.

I felt unusually tired at dinner and my forehead was burning up a little, but I just assumed I was tired from Gardening as that was tough work. Bryan and I locked eyes across the dining area.

Was he really that different or would I just end up hurting him too? I wondered.

27

The clinic

A couple of days later, I had received an email from my lawyer:

Dear Miss Sheldon,

Thank you for your email about the two boys that your friends, Emily and Nicole, had spoken to at the party. They will be brought into questioning.

I would also like to inform you that the forensic reports detected a substance called strychnine which is poisonous, and it is believed to be the cause of death for Robbie Wilson.

If you are able to recall any more information, please do let me know.

Kind regards,
Charlie Grant

Strychnine? Who would bring poison to a party? What about the dagger in his chest? Unless the dagger was… inserted… after he was already dead? Which means someone was using the dagger as a cover up… But did they persuade me to do it? I was pretty drunk that night. So many questions circulated my mind.

At Gardening, Adamson turned on the water fountain for the pond and released some goldfish. We all cheered with pride at what we accomplished in just a matter of days. He then took us to the vegetable garden where all sorts of vegetables were grown for the kitchen to use. He explained the essentials we needed to know about growing and maintaining crops. He then put us to work of gathering up any vegetables that were ready to be harvested. I knelt down to the ground and worked on the potato patch. I started to feel very drowsy and my forehead was burning hot. Chichi noticed that I was struggling and asked:

'Lottie, are you ok?'

'Um… I'm not sure, I feel like fainting.'

Chichi started to look worried.

'Ok, just wait here and don't do anything. I'm going to get Adamson.'

She hurried off to get Adamson who said:

'Please go to the clinic immediately. Chichi, please go with her.'

As Chichi and I walked over to the clinic. I asked her:

'What's happening to me, Chichi?'

'I can't know for sure, but I think you might have malaria,' she said nervously.

'What? No! Am I going to die?'

'No, don't worry. The clinic will know how to treat it, it's very common.'

I felt as pale as a ghost by the time we arrived at the clinic. Chichi described my symptoms to the nurse. I was taken to have a blood test and then, the nurse took me to a room with a small bed to lie on. About twenty minutes later, the doctor came in and explained:

'Lottie, your blood test results were positive for malaria and you'll be kept here till you recover. We've phoned your mum and she's on her way.'

The nurse connected my arm to a drip with some kind of medicine to pump through me. I gradually started to feel quite sleepy till I fell asleep... *We were just heading to the drinks station, when one of the boys I recognised from Robbie's group of friends stopped us.*

'Robbie! Where have you been man?'

Was I invisible? I asked myself.

'Sorry Lewis, I'm on a date tonight,' Robbie said.

'Oh right, ok.'

One of the strange looking boys that Emily and Nicole were talking to earlier approached us.

'You boys been to the real party yet?'

'What do you mean, dude?' Lewis asked.

'The attic. VIPs only. You interested?'

'Hell yeah. Robbie, you and your date coming or what?'

'Um...'

He looked at me and I nodded.

'Yeah, we'll come.'

We all headed upstairs. The boy who invited us pulled down a step ladder from the ceiling and began climbing up. We followed suit to find a few couches, a small coffee table with lines of white powder and rolled-up pieces of paper. There were more bottles of alcohol available. I was surprised to find Emily and Nicole there. Is this where they had disappeared to?

My eyes crept open to find Mother sitting by my side, just watching me. She smiled and said:

'Hello, sweetheart.'

'Hi, Mum.'

She stroked my hair.

'I spoke to the doctor and he explained that you have malaria, so they'll keep you here till you recover. But don't worry Lottie, they know very well how to treat malaria here. I remember having it as a child many years ago.'

'Oh, I had no idea. What have you been doing while I've been here at camp anyway?'

'Well, I've been catching up with some of my friends from my old school days, been doing my best to stay updated about the investigation and I've also been doing some volunteer work in some of the local villages.'

'I got the email from Charlie about the forensic reports.'

'Oh, I hadn't realised you were copied on that. What do you think of it?'

'I think someone either convinced me or inserted the dagger to cover up his death somehow.'

'What are you talking about, sweetheart?'

'When I woke up next to him… he had a dagger in his chest.'

'I see… Did you touch it?'

'Yeah, I used it to lift myself up.'

'Oh Lottie, that means your DNA is all over it!'

'Mum, I didn't know what I was touching at the time!'

She took a deep breath.

'Just rest for now… This stress isn't good for your health…

I'm sure we'll figure a way out of this.'

Throughout the next few days, my bunkmates as well as Chichi made sure to visit me in the mornings during Leisure time. Bryan never came which concerned me. Did he care about me at all? It didn't matter anyway as I was enjoying spending time with Mother as I hadn't seen her since she dropped me off at the airport.

'So, how's camp going so far?'

'Pretty good actually. I'm glad you sent me here, it's quite different to what I had imagined.'

'Your friends seem really nice.'

'Better than Nicole and Emily.'

'It's just as difficult for them as it is for you, Lottie.'

'Do you think I did it, Mum?'

'I'm praying you didn't.'

'It was our first date.'

'Yes, but there were alcohol and drugs too.'

'I just wanted to fit in… and impress Robbie.'

Was I really the one that killed Robbie that night? I searched for an answer to that question but was yet to find an answer.

28

Forensics

Did you hear about the forensics report? N x
Yeah, I got Lottie's message… I thought you weren't talking to me? E x
I'm not but I think this could help you… N x
How so? E x
You said he was already dead before you tried framing Lottie? N x

I sat on my bed thinking and then got up to head out of the house to find Chip who was in his usual alleyway for "business" purposes.

'Chip! I need to talk to you!'

He gave his buddy, Paul, a thumbs-up which was his signal for him to take over while he talked to me and then jogged towards me.

'You got five minutes before my next client arrives.'

'Forensics discovered a poison called strychnine in the drug that killed Robbie.'

'Sweet! That means we're off the hook for his death then!'

'Chip, do you not realise how serious this? Why would you give him poison?'

'Oh, you think I knew there was poison in the cocaine. How was I supposed to know? To me, it just looked like any other cocaine I've bought before.'

'Well, it might be worth getting to know who your suppliers are! And I want you to know that as soon as Lottie is back from her summer camp, I'm telling the police the truth... about everything.'

'You little cow. And you call yourself my girlfriend?'

'I *was* your girlfriend but we're officially over now.'

'I'll see you in prison, babe.'

'Lottie is my best friend and I'm not gonna let her go to prison for something she didn't do.'

'We'll see about that.'

I walked away and texted Nicole:

I broke up with Chip and I've decided I'll tell the police the whole truth when Lottie is back, but I was wondering if you would both come with me because I could really use the support? E x

Of course, we will. I'm proud of you. N x

That Michelle on the phone was right, there was still time for me to change things around. I had the biggest smile on my face knowing that I was doing the right thing, even if meant I would probably get sent to jail for it.

29

Truth or Dare?

O n Friday afternoon, we left camp for our last excursion which was Mumbo Island. The bus ride was pleasantly short as we arrived at Kayak Africa in less than two hours. We were greeted by a confident surfer type called James who explained that we would be taking a speed boat to the island. They also gave us snorkelling masks and snorkels. We all excitedly jumped into the speed boat waiting for our next adventure. As we approached Mumbo Island, a very sandy beach with tropical blue waters surrounding it appeared. There was a pile of kayaks on the beach just waiting for us to use as well as a really long wooden bridge that connected a smaller island with the bigger island. James led us to the smaller island via the bridge. There were six small chalets that looked similar to what we stayed in at Liwonde, an outdoor dining area and an outdoor shower. It was already 5:30pm so, our instructors told us that there would be no swimming under any circumstances till tomorrow morning.

Once we settled into our chalets, we were told to spray

ourselves with mosquito spray which I obeyed given I didn't want to face having malaria again. Then, the other girls and I headed down the bridge back towards the beach for dinner. There were several small tables and camper chairs set up for dinner which was barbecue chicken with fried rice followed by banana cake for pudding. After dinner, a bunch of us sat by the fire on the beach. It was so toasty and warm, perfect for looking at the stars above in the dark night sky. Sam suggested:

'Anyone want to play Truth or Dare?'

Truth or Dare! That was what we did up in the attic as I recalled…

'Are there any mixers I can use for my drink?' I asked.

'Rule number one: no mixers allowed. Only spirits,' Chip said.

'You mean we have to drink pure alcohol, all night?'

'Yup, got a problem with that?'

'Nope.'

I always hated peer pressure as he poured vodka into my plastic red cup.

'Birthday girl, Truth or Dare?' he asked.

'Dare,' Nicole responded.

'I dare you to kiss one of the girls.'

'Easy.'

She leaned towards Emily and they shared a kiss. How much had the two of them drunk? I wondered as I took a sip of my vodka, it tasted awful.

'Lottie, Truth or Dare?' Nicole asked.

'Truth.'

'Oh, come on, live a little.'

She was definitely drunk.

'Fine, Dare.'

'Dare you to down your drink.'

'But it's solid vodka?'

'Can't refuse a Dare.'

I lifted my cup to my lips and let the vodka slither and burn down my throat. I wanted to throw-up.

'Excuse me, I need the bathroom.'

'Knew you couldn't handle it,' Emily chimed.

Nicole laughed alongside her. Were they trying to impress someone?

I stood up from the couches and headed towards the step ladder but just as I was climbing down, I heard someone ask.

'Bryan, Truth or Dare?'

'Dare.'

'Dare you to snort a line on the table.'

I watched as he picked up a rolled-up piece of paper, put it near his nose and bent towards the table to snort the powder up his nose like it wasn't his first time. Before I could comment, the vomit was rising up towards my lips, so I quickly dashed down the step ladder for the bathroom.

'Lottie?' Sam asked.

'Hhmm… what?'

'Are you playing?'

'Yeah, sure.'

I continued staring at the fire burning the firewood as I wondered who was the *real* Robbie Wilson? He was popular, insanely attractive, the top athlete at our school, he was in the year above but although that makes him look good on paper, there wasn't anything I really knew about him as a person other than the fact that he liked playing computer games. Did he struggle with anything? Was he under a lot of pressure? Did he have any enemies? There was only one person I knew who could answer my questions… Bryan.

30

Secrets

We woke up early the next morning and got ourselves ready for the day. The instructors gathered us up for a quick meeting before we had breakfast. They handed us a list of possible activities to choose from which included *kayaking, snorkelling, swimming, relaxing on the beach, boa* and *walks around the island (must have a guide or instructor with you)*.

Chichi and I decided we wanted to start with Kayaking as that's not something we could do at camp. We decided to take two single kayaks as we felt it would be more fun than a double one. Neither of us had ever kayaked before but it sounded easy enough. The man said we were allowed to go around the whole island if we wanted to as long as we didn't venture too far away from the actual island. That certainly sounded like a challenge worth doing! Chichi and I practised a little just to get the hang of it first and then, we set off around the smaller island to see what we could find. The water below us was a mix of various shades of blue and transparent enough to see everything below us from colourful fishes to big gigantic rocks. I looked over at Chichi and she knew exactly what I was thinking of; we definitely had to go snorkelling later.

On our left, we soon came across a big dark cave and we were curious as to what we might find in it. As we approached the cave, we noticed lots of little white dots staring at us, we wondered what they might be when out of the blue, several black bats came flying towards us. We screamed as we ducked down whilst they flew past us. Once they had got past, we turned the kayaks around to head back.

Just before lunch, we found Chabata and Thoko swimming in the lake and we decided to join them. Chabata saw us and said:

'Oh hey! How did you find the kayaking?'

I replied:

'It was so good, but you should avoid the cave near that small part of the island up ahead, it's got bats in it!'

'Oh no! Well, thanks for the tip, I might try it after lunch.'

Lunch was the classic chambo and chips; the best fish and chips I'd ever tasted.

Chichi asked me:

'So, what's going on with you and Bryan? I haven't seen you spend much time with him lately.'

'Last time we spoke, he said he needed space to process the Luwawa incident, but he never visited me while I was at the clinic so maybe, he's just lost interest in me.'

'Yeah, he's always been bad at communicating his feelings,' Chabata commented.

'What do you mean?'

'Well, when I was his girlfriend...'

I interrupted.

'Wait, you two are exes?'

'Yeah, we dated for like two summers but it never quite worked out once camp was over, didn't he tell you?'

'No, he said you were good camp friends.'

I got up and stormed towards the beach looking to clear my head to find Joyce sitting close enough to the lake water to touch her feet. I sat down next to her and asked:

'Mind if I join you?'

'Of course, you can.'

'What are you thinking about?'

'I'm worried about my family.'

'Oh, have you heard from them lately?'

'My mother has been battling HIV all summer whilst I've been selfishly having the time of my life here at camp, which is just as well as my father has found someone for me to have an arranged marriage with once the camp finishes.'

'But you're so young… You have no need to do that yet in your life.'

'It's part of my culture, you wouldn't understand… What's on your mind?'

'I might get sent to prison when I get back to the UK.'

'What? Why? I don't understand.'

'They think I killed this boy at a party I went to back in England.'

She shifted slightly towards her right.

'Please don't be scared, I was trying to keep it a secret as I was worried no one would want to be my friend here otherwise.'

'I noticed you've been sleep-talking quite a bit lately.'

'Yeah, I keep trying to re-trace what happened that night.'

'Do you think you did it?'

'I was on a first date with him… but a lot of alcohol was consumed so… I just don't understand why I would do that even if I was insanely drunk… But I woke up the next day to find him lying next to me… dead… with a dagger in his chest.'

'Sorry, I shouldn't have asked.'

'He did snort a drug that night as a Dare… I saw him do it and a bunch of us including me drank pure alcohol without any mixer and I remember how sick it made me feel.'

'That sounds complicated…What about your friends? Did they see anything?'

'They were acting weird that night… I had completely forgotten we were meant to go get our hair and make-up done before the party and instead went on a date with Robbie so… I guess they were upset about that… They could have at least talked to me first before handing me over to the police.'

'Perhaps they were scared?'

'I suppose.'

Later that day, Chabata told me that Bryan was looking for me and asked if I'd meet him on the beach after dinner to talk so I did. He had his hands in his jean pockets with his shoulders raised like our encounter wasn't awkward enough already.

'Hey, Lottie.'

'Hey.'

'I'm sorry we haven't talked in a while… How are you?'

'I'm alright, thanks.'

'Okay. There's something I need to tell you about that night in the forest.'

'Yeah?'

'I lied to you about how I found Josh… I did trip over something and collapse to the ground, but Josh somehow found me and woke me up…'

'Okay and?'

'Well, while we walked back towards the campsite, we got talking and he told me he fancied you.'

He waited for a reaction from me before continuing on.

'I tried to laugh it off but then… He said he knew you had feelings for him too… Cause you kissed him at that disco we had a few weeks back.'

I knew I should have told him about that kiss.

'I only did that because I was upset about you and Chabata's kiss… it didn't mean anything.'

'Why didn't you tell me though?'

'Well, why didn't you tell me that Chabata is your ex?'

'How do you know about that?'

'She happened to mention it.'

He sighed.

'That night was a final goodbye kiss as I told her I was interested in you.'

'Why was Josh so badly injured and in a ditch?'

'I got mad and jealous I suppose… So, we ended up having a fistfight but as it was dark… We couldn't see very well, and I accidentally pushed him into a ditch.'

'So, you got into a fight all because I kissed a boy when you weren't even my boyfriend? Unbelievable honestly.'

'Well it's not like he's dead.'

'That's not fair! I'm trying so hard to recall what happened to Robbie.'

'Well, have you made any progress?'

'Some… But clearly you think I did it!'

I stormed off back to my chalet before he could say another

word. It was getting harder to believe that I could be inno-cent… First, Mother, and now Bryan believed I was guilty.

31

Kulingana Colour Festival

Once we were back at camp, Emma came into the bunk wearing some kind of warrior outfit made up of fabrics and plastic items put together. She pranced about the room shouting:

'IT'S TIME FOR CAMP KULINGANA'S COLOUR FESTIVAL! ARE YOU READY!?'

We were rushed out of the bunks, still in our pyjamas and directed towards the stage. I was completely puzzled as to what was happening, but the others were very excited about this announcement. Tony and Mayamiko appeared on the stage. Everyone was cheering with excitement. Tony spoke out on the microphone.

'Good morning everybody! We've just announced the most exciting and best part of camp which is the KULINGANA COLOUR FESTIVAL!'

The crowd erupted with more cheers and excitement.

'For those of you who have no idea as to what that means, it's our camp tradition where we split up the whole camp into four colours; Blue, Green, Red and Yellow. You'll all take part in various fun activities and have the chance to score some points for your teams! And the best part is that it lasts a WHOLE WEEK! Now head back to your bunks and GOOD LUCK TO ALL THE TEAMS, LET YOUR COLOURS BRIGHTEN THE SKIES!'

We dashed back to the bunk filled with excitement. I was put into the Blue team with Joyce, Thoko and Amy were put into the Green team, Samantha was put into the Red team and Chabata was put into the Yellow team. We were all given a t-shirt in our team colours and encouraged to wear as much of our team colour as possible. Emma also had face-paint for all of us to wear. Whilst we were getting dressed up, I noticed Joyce was sitting on her bed looking down at the ground with her blue shirt still in her right-hand. I asked:

'Hey Joyce, you can have my blue beaded bracelet if you're struggling to find blue things to wear?'

'I don't care about the Colour Festival.'

'Oh, I think it's going to be a lot of fun.'

Joyce suddenly burst into tears. The others immediately rushed over. I put a hand on Joyce's back and asked:

'Joyce, are you ok?'

'My mum is dying, and I'm stuck here when I should be with her!'

I'd forgotten about that; she needed a friend just as much as I did, but my brain went numb just thinking of things to say or do to comfort her. Thoko spoke up and said:

'Joyce, we're all here for you. We might not be able to feel your pain exactly but we're not leaving your side.'

'Thanks, Thoko.'

Chabata added:

'You're so incredibly brave, Joyce. You've been here for what? Six weeks already? Your mum would be so proud of you to see what you've accomplished here. When we leave this place, we have to battle our own problems in the world but when we're here, we don't have to worry about those problems, we can just be who we want to be. It's a way of healing.'

Joyce's tears were starting to fade.

'I don't know what came over me. I just worry about her and I miss her so much.'

We all gave her a group hug.

'Right, we're gonna add a little sparkle and then, go out there and make the Blue team proud in those swimming relays... for your mum,' I said.

'Thanks, Lottie. That means a lot.'

'You're welcome, Joyce. Let's go make your mum even prouder of you.'

We sat on the benches in our house colours. There were all sorts of races, short, long, different strokes and even a four-person relay at the end. Joyce signed up for the front crawl race against Chichi who was Green, Maria who was Red and Mercy who was Yellow. I stood as close to the pool side-line as I could. The whistle went so, the girls all dived in and set off. I screamed as loud as I could:

'GO JOYCE! YOU CAN DO IT!'

Joyce started to tread water halfway through the race in panic. I ran and safely dived into the pool till I was by her side. I hugged her and said:

'You can do it, Joyce! We'll do it together, it's not much further to the end.'

'I don't know if I can reach the end.'

'Yes, you can. Remember, we're doing this for your mum, and I'll be right here next to you.'

'Okay, let's do it.'

Joyce and I continued swimming to the end. The crowds applauded which encouraged us to keep going until we finally reached the end. As we both got out of the pool, Emma wrapped us both in giant blue towels. She said:

'Well done, girls.'

'Thanks, Emma.'

Just before dinner, Tony made an announcement with the microphone.

'What a brilliant start to our Kulingana Colour Festival! I hope everyone enjoyed those relays because from what I saw, everyone tried their hardest to score some points for their teams. Well, remember this is just the start! There is plenty more to come! But here are the total scores so far. In fourth place, we have Yellow with a total of thirty points!'

The yellow team cheered and applauded.

'Then, in third place, we have Blue with forty points!'

My team cheered and applauded even louder than the Yellows.

'Now, it was very close for first place... drum roll please.'

Everyone started tapping their thighs to make a drumming noise.

'In first place, we have Green with fifty points followed by Red with forty-five points!'

The Greens went ecstatic with their cheers and applauds. This was just the start, we'll catch up to them, I was sure of that. I confidently told myself.

That night, I remembered that *I had noticed Robbie was trembling and cradling his head as though he was about to throw-up.*

'*Bobbie! Are... Are you all right?*'

'*Yeah, I'll be fine... I just need the bathroom... I'll be back in just a few minutes.*'

'*Ok! Don't take too long though!*'

I watched Robbie go down the stairs but then, every now and then, I checked my phone for the time which was 21:30... 21:37... 21:43. Robbie still hadn't returned so, I decided to go check on him. As I got off the sofa, I started seeing everything and everyone in double and I could hardly walk straight. I wondered if that was when he reacted to the strychnine? He did take his time in the bathroom after all.

32

Emergency bunk meeting

For the next two days, we had a mini-Olympics. The first day consisted of football, basketball and volleyball matches. The second was all about ultimate frisbee, hockey and athletics. Joyce radiated positive energy, but I suspected it was to stop the rest of us from worrying about her. As we were walking to the football pitches for ultimate frisbee. I asked:

'How are you feeling today?'

'Yeah, much better thanks. Just trying to keep myself distracted.'

'I know the feeling. When was the last time you heard from her?'

'Just before we went to Mumbo Island. We weren't able to speak for long as talking tires her out, but my dad said she's not looking well.'

She burst into tears again. I hugged her and let her cry. I just wished I could think of some way to help her. Once Joyce calmed down. I set off to try and find Emma, who was in the office filling out some forms. She was surprised to see me and said:

'Lottie, is everything ok? You know you're meant to be at the football pitches for frisbee, right?'

'Yeah, I know. I just… I just need to talk to you about something.'

'Of course, what's up?'

'I'm worried about Joyce.'

'I know, I am too. It's not looking good for her mum, but we just have to keep praying and do whatever we can to comfort her.'

'I just feel so useless. Is there anything we can do to help her?'

Emma sighed and took a moment to think of something till she thought of an idea.

'I think I might know something we can do.'

I followed Emma to find out.

That night, we had an outdoor movie night, my body needed it as I was aching all over. I sat next to Chichi who whispered:

'Where have you been? I haven't seen you all day?'

'I've been trying to support Joyce as her mum has HIV.'

'Oh, I'm sorry to hear that, hope she'll be ok.'

'There's something I've been meaning to talk to you about actually.'

'Oh yeah?'

'Chichi, you've been an amazing friend to me all summer… I'm very grateful for that but there's something you need to know about me.'

'Ok… what is it?'

'I'm a suspect in a murder investigation back in England.'

'WHAT?' She yelled.

A few heads turned towards us.

'Sorry.'

They turned back towards the movie.

'What? Why didn't you tell me?' She whispered.

'I wanted to… I just didn't think you'd want to be my friend.'

'What happened?'

'I was on a date with this boy I'd been crushing on at school and it was my best… my friend's birthday party that night, which we both went to but there were these strange looking boys I'd never seen at school before who arranged a 'VIP' party up in the attic, where there were drugs, and everyone was forced to drink pure alcohol… I didn't take any of the drugs, but I did drink a lot, Robbie did both… Anyway, I woke up the next day and he… he was… he was dead… Then, before I had a chance to process what had happened… I got arrested.'

'Does the camp know about this?'

'No… My therapist pulled some strings and convinced the police this would help me with my mental health as I just… my mind went completely blank about that night… but being here has really helped me face what happened.'

'Did you do it?'

'There was a forensic report that stated his death was caused from the drugs which makes me think someone put the dagger in his chest as a cover-up… I don't think I would have done that no matter how drunk I was… but no one seems to believe I could be innocent.'

'That's a lot to take in but thank you for telling me, I completely understand why you would keep that quiet though so there's no hard feelings.'

Suddenly I felt a tap on my shoulder.

'Lottie.'

I turned around to find Emma who continued saying.

'Grab the others, we're having an emergency bunk meeting NOW!'

I got up and gathered up the other Bunk Madzi girls. I couldn't find Joyce anywhere though which made me panic a little till we arrived at the bunk to find her crying. Emma calmly said:

'Sorry to interrupt the movie, girls, but I have some very sad news to share.'

We all sat down in a circle. I had a bad feeling about what was going to happen as Emma said:

'We just got a call that Joyce's Mum passed away an hour ago. She'll be leaving tomorrow morning for the funeral and she could do with some support right now.'

We gathered together in a group hug as Joyce shed her tears. She needed our support and that was all that mattered that night.

33

Game over

It was the last official day of camp and Joyce was sadly leaving early for the funeral. We gave her one more group hug before she got into the car. Emma and I brought out ten kilos of maize in a white straw bag for her. Joyce was speechless. I said:

'I wanted to do something to help you, Joyce. Emma told me that Malawians give the grieving family some maize for the funeral to feed everyone. I just hope this is enough for you and your family.'

Joyce pulled me into a hug and said:

'Thank you, Lottie. This means a lot and you've done more than enough to help me, thank you. Also, I'm sticking by your side, no matter what happens with that investigation.'

'Thank you, I really appreciate that.'

She said her goodbyes to everyone and then got into the car and set off. It was like a piece of us was missing as we continued on with our day.

That night, all the teams would be performing a song of their choice in front of a few judges who would finalise the Colour

Festival winners! We had the whole day to practice and our team captains were very excited to get going…

Battle of the Songs finally began. I was a little nervous about our performance. Red were up first, and they did a cover of 'Dance like Crazy' by Macaroons. They were good but we were next. We walked onto the stage and formed a horseshoe shape just like we had practiced earlier. We created an original song based on the tune of 'Can't stop the feeling' by Justin Timberlake which went like this:

'We're here as campers who sleep in bunks.
It's pretty cool, when you go for a swim.
Then, play some football, in the sun.
We're having fun, nothing more, till it's done.
We got that dance class in the morning.
Where we kick off to a beat.
Camp Kulingana, here we go!
Say cheese. Cheese!
The staff are pretty cool, we just can't go to sleep.
So, we sneak out to the beach. Wait, what?'
Under the stars, while everyone sleeps.
We have a chat, just you and me, please.
There're no instructors, we are free.
So, just listen, just listen, just listen…
Camp Kulingana, we are here to just sing, sing, sing.
Battle of the Songs, will you just please, please, please.
Clap your hands and click to the beat, beat, beat.
We have just won this battle, no exceptions.'

The crowd went absolutely crazy for our song which proved

to be a true winner. But was it enough to improve our Colour Festival score? Once Green and Yellow did their performances, the judges stepped outside to discuss the final Colour Festival results. I was practically biting my nails, just thinking about the results until the judges had returned.

'We just want to start by saying that those performances were brilliant! They were all so good that it made our decision ten times harder to pick a winner. But the show must go on and here's the moment you've all been waiting for... drum roll please.'

The room erupted with an energising drumbeat.

'In fourth place, we have Yellow with two hundred points! Well done to them!'

'In third place, we have Green with three hundred and fifty points! Well done!'

'Now first place was very, very close with these last two teams. In first place, we have... Blue with four hundred and fifty points and in second place, we have Red with four hundred and twenty points!'

I couldn't believe it, our team actually won! This victory was for you Joyce. I said to myself as though she could hear me.

34

'Tell me everything.'

With our suitcases packed, bed linen stripped off and our bunks cleaned for the last time. We sat in the dining area till our parents came to pick us up or the various buses to the airport departed.

'I can't believe camp is over, it went by so fast.'

'I know the feeling. Do you think you'll be back next year?' Chichi asked.

'I hope so... It just depends on this investigation really.'

'Well, I hope you'll be able to come back cause it's the last chance we have to be campers.'

Mother stepped out of a small blue hire car she drove in and gave me a wave to catch my attention.

'That's my cue to leave, I'm gonna miss you a lot Chichi, promise we'll stay in touch?'

'Of course! You have my details.'

I gave her a massive hug and quickly went around to say goodbye to my other friends. Then, I headed to the car for Mother to take me home.

'Hello sweetheart, ready to go home?'

'Hi Mum, yeah I am, though, I am going to miss this place.'

'I'm so glad you ended up liking Camp Kulingana. Now, seatbelt on, so we can go home.'

As we drove along, I watched the villages, children, cattle go by till my eyes shut for a nap where…

'Wha… Where… Where is he?' I asked.

'Let's check the bathrooms,' Emily suggested.

We walked straight ahead towards the closest bathroom. I knocked on the door and shouted:

'Robbie! Are you in there?'

There was no response. So, I tried opening the door handle but the door was locked.

'Wha… What do… What do we do?'

'Wait, I'll get Chip.'

'Chip? No, Bobbie is stuck… I don't want to eat chips.'

'Look, here is he.'

Chip, the party leader arrived.

'Oh, your name is Chip! What a weird name that is!'

'Lottie, do you want his help or not?'

'Yeah! Open the door!'

'All right, move out my way.'

Emily and I stepped aside as Chip ran towards the door with a blurry object and the door opened. I ran inside to find Robbie cradled by the toilet basin with vomit coming out of his mouth. He seemed motionless.

'Robbie!'

Then, everything suddenly turned dark as I collapsed to the floor.

I jerked myself awake, gathering my thoughts about where

I was exactly. I looked towards Mother.

'Bad dream, sweetheart?' She asked.

I started to cry.

'Lottie! What happened?'

She pulled the car over to one side, undid her seat belt and cradled me towards her chest.

'I didn't do it, Mum… I didn't kill Robbie.'

'Tell me everything.'

And so, I did.

35

The price for the truth

I stopped just outside the police station. Nicole arrived five minutes later and said:

'Welcome back, Lottie! How was camp?'

'Thanks Nicole, it was quite an adventure but a lot of fun. I got your message.'

'I figured you did cause why else would you be here. You know she's been suffering all summer about what she did right?'

'So, have I. I only just figured it out myself a few days ago. Where is she anyway?'

'I don't know. She said she would meet us here.'

'Do you think she changed her mind? Cause I'm telling them if she doesn't.'

'Give her a chance. She's probably just running late. I'll give her a call.'

Nicole dialled her number, but it went straight to voicemail.

'Maybe her phone died?'

'I'm not wasting any more time on this.'

I started walking up the stairs and opened the door to find

Mrs Greene, Emily's mum on the other side.

'Mrs Greene? What are you doing here?' I asked.

'Oh Lottie, my little Emily has gone missing! I've just reported to the police as it's been forty-eight hours and we've tried ringing her mobile, but it just goes to voicemail each time. Have you heard from her?'

'Oh Mrs Greene. I'm so sorry, no I haven't. Nicole and I were actually meant to meet her here at the station, but she never came.'

'Why would she be meeting you girls at the police station?'

'She didn't tell you, did she?'

'Tell me, what?'

'She was involved with that boy who died at Nicole's birthday party and she was ready to confess today but wanted me and Nicole there for support.'

'My little Emily wouldn't do such a thing! She's a very good girl!'

'I know Mrs Greene. It was an accident. Let's go back inside and inform the police on what I've just told you as it might help them find her and we will find her Mrs Greene, we won't stop till we do.'

'Thank you so much, girls. You were both very important people to her.'

We entered the station together.

Emily, wherever you are, we're coming to get you.

THE END.

About the author

Ashling Bourke is half Finnish and half Irish but was born and raised in Malawi. She attended an international school there and was surrounded by a diverse range of cultures and nationalities, which very much influenced the atmosphere demonstrated at Camp Kulingana. She has worked in both an American summer camp and a British summer camp, and also did her dissertation research at The University of Stirling on British summer camps. She found that there was a lot of interest in her upbringing in Malawi, just from meeting others for the very first time, which inspired her to write her novel *Innocently Guilty* to promote Malawi and encourage readers to experience The Warm Heart of Africa.

Acknowledgements

I have had an incredibly positive experience with The Conrad Press and James Essinger has not only supported me and guided me throughout the entire publication process, but he has also shared valuable writing advice that will never be forgotten.

I would also like to thank Charlotte Mouncey for designing an exceptional front cover and ensuring *Innocently Guilty* is at the highest professional standard possible.

I would also like to thank my mum who was there for me from beginning to end throughout the whole writing experience and told me to never give up on my writing.

Lastly, I would like to thank my readers for reading and encouraging me to write even more and for being a part of the journey too.